# TO LOVE AGAIN

Meg and her little daughter Katie flee to rural Devon to escape her sinister ex-husband Phillip. Here Meg meets the reclusive artist Garth Winter, and although neither wants to become friends they cannot ignore the magnetism between them. As the threat from Phillip increases, Meg realises she needs Garth's help to keep Katie safe. Set against a backdrop of country moors and busy London streets, Meg must battle to keep her daughter while she falls irresistibly in love with Garth.

*Books by Carol MacLean*
*in the Linford Romance Library:*

WILD FOR LOVE
RESCUE MY HEART
RETURN TO BARRADALE
THE JUBILEE LETTER
FROZEN HEART
JUNGLE FEVER

CAROL MacLEAN

# TO LOVE AGAIN

*Complete and Unabridged*

LINFORD
*Leicester*

First published in Great Britain in 2014

First Linford Edition
published 2015

A catalogue record for this book is available
from the British Library.

ISBN 978–1–4448–2262–5

Published by
F. A. Thorpe (Publishing)
Anstey, Leicestershire

Set by Words & Graphics Ltd.
Anstey, Leicestershire
Printed and bound in Great Britain by
T. J. International Ltd., Padstow, Cornwall

This book is printed on acid-free paper

# 1

*We'll be safe here*, was Meg's first thought on seeing the thatched cottage. It lay at the end of a short lane, with the fields behind it patchwork-perfect and a woodland copse on the gentle slope beyond. She was dusty and tired after the long drive from north London and the gleaming white walls of her new home looked clean and fresh, promising a new start for both of them.

She turned back to her Ford Fiesta, which she'd parked badly across the lane. Still, it was a dead end apart from a rusted gate into a field, so no one was going to want to get past. Inside the car Katie slept, her head at an angle to her neck and a smear of chocolate on her mouth. Meg struggled to lift her. At three, Katie was already getting too heavy for her to carry. The little girl didn't wake and somehow Meg managed to

1

turn the key in the lock of the cottage door and get inside, where she laid her daughter on a couch in the room on the left. Then she explored, taking her time, enjoying the sensation of doing things at her own pace with no one else to command her.

The cottage was in good condition and had recently been painted, Meg noted with relief. The last thing she wanted was to have to decorate her new home. She was happy to simply move her few pieces of furniture in and start living here. The house had an air of peacefulness which welcomed her. Outside there was birdsong and bright late-summer sunshine trickling in through a window that had been left open to freshen the room. Meg grinned. In London no windows were ever left open if the house was empty. But here in rural Devon, it was all right. That cheered her. The last of her doubts dissolved and she felt herself relax. She'd done the right thing.

The roar of a throaty engine broke the peace. There was the screech of poorly applied brakes and Meg peered out of the tiny bedroom window and smiled. Tabby had arrived. She clattered down the narrow wooden staircase, ducking unnecessarily under the low beam, and got to the door just as it swung open.

'Meg, darling, you made it!' Tabby rushed forward and hugged her affectionately. Then she pushed Meg back and scrunched up her eyes to really look at her. 'Too thin, darling girl, too thin by half. Not to worry, that'll be solved after a few Devon high teas. I'll pop along later with a pot of the local clotted cream. It's delicious — have you ever tried it? I can't get William to stop eating the stuff.'

Meg let her friend's chatter envelop her and steered Tabby to the kitchen, nodding in the right places and waiting until Tabby had talked out her welcome. There was a big old battered table and four chairs with faded blue cushions. An old-fashioned Belfast sink stood under the window and a black range took up one whole wall. She found a kettle and filled it, but then wondered how to heat it.

Tabby took it from her and lifted a lid on the range top. She put the kettle on the hot circle. 'The range is lit. I got Maurice to come down and sort it out and I've put in some crockery and cutlery just 'til you get yourself sorted. Don't worry, you'll soon learn to use a range, city girl,' she teased. 'Oh, Meg, I'm so glad you decided to come down here to live. It's going to be wonderful.'

A momentary darkness shadowed Meg's heart. She hoped Tabby was right, but the sheer ordinariness of her surroundings made her feel her fears were foolish and she forced her muscles to relax. 'I can't thank you enough for telling me about the cottage,' she said. 'I think Katie and I will be very happy here.'

'Well, London's no place to bring up a small child, is it?' Tabby shuddered. 'A horrid place with dirty air and no space to run about.'

But Meg felt a fleeting tug of sadness at the thought of London. She was a city girl through and through. She loved the hustle and bustle of the busy streets and the noise of the traffic. It was what she was used to. She'd moved to London as a teenager to get away from the small northern town she'd grown up in, and had lived and worked there ever since.

'Of course, you had that lovely house in Kew and were lucky to have Kew Gardens as your playground,' Tabby went on. 'But it must have been quite different when you had to move to Tottenham.'

Meg bit her lip and turned away, fussing with the blue and white milk jug and matching mugs. The terror of her flight from her home in Kew to the grimy flat in Tottenham rose up like bile. It threatened to poison the sweet air in Primrose Cottage. She fumbled with the mugs and one slipped from her grasp and shattered on the flagged tiles.

'Oh Meg, I'm so sorry. Me and my

big mouth,' Tabby cried, rushing to pick up the shards. 'Maurice is always telling me to watch what I'm saying. That was thoughtless. Of course you don't want to think about Phillip. Don't mind me. Please say you forgive me, darling.'

'It's okay.' Meg managed a smile, kneeling down to help gather the last bits of china. 'I'd rather not talk about it though, if you don't mind.'

'Mummy,' Katie called from the other room.

Meg went to get her. Katie rubbed her eyes sleepily. She needed a bath after their long journey. Meg hoped Tabby's husband Maurice had managed to arrange hot water too.

'Did you have a nice sleep, sweetie?' Meg kissed the top of her daughter's soft head. She smelt of biscuits and chocolate and clammy sleep.

Katie nodded.

'This is Auntie Tabby,' Meg said, carrying her through to the kitchen where Tabby had restored order and made another pot of tea.

'My, haven't you grown?' Tabby said fondly, giving the child a kiss.

Katie cuddled in to her mother shyly, hiding in the crook of Meg's neck and watching Tabby out of one eye.

'You don't remember me but I'm your mummy's best friend,' Tabby told her. 'The last time I saw you, you were just a tiny baby.'

Meg felt ashamed. Tabby was her best friend, and had been most of her life since school days, yet she'd met Katie only once. Phillip had made sure of that.

'I've got a little girl too,' Tabby chatted on. 'My little girl's called Jane and she's five. I'm sure the two of you will be great friends.'

'Is she an only girl?' Katie whispered, still nestled close to Meg.

'Jane's got a big sister, Ellen, who's eleven tomorrow, and two big brothers — Jacob, who's thirteen, and William, who's eight.'

'Oh,' Katie said, the longing was clear in her voice.

Meg cuddled her, guilt flushing her again. It was a weariness, feeling that way. Wasn't it part of the reason for fleeing to the south coast? Part of her fresh start was to feel good about herself. Phillip had never wanted children. When Katie came along he was adamant that she was to be an only child. Meg should've fought harder for a brother or sister for her. Never mind that she never won a battle with Phillip, and in the end, she'd lost the war.

'Is Ellen having a party?' Katie asked with interest. She wriggled free from Meg's clasp and climbed onto the chair next to Tabby, her chubby little legs swinging from it.

'If you knew Ellen, you wouldn't have to ask that,' Tabby laughed. 'She's a real party animal. Would you like to come to help us celebrate tomorrow?'

'Yes, please.' Katie clapped her hands in glee.

'I don't know, Katie kid,' Meg said hesitantly. 'Maybe we need a couple of days to settle in here.'

Her instinct was to hide away, but Tabby was having none of it.

'I'll help you get sorted but there's loads of time to do that,' Tabby said. 'You must both come to Ellen's party tomorrow and meet your neighbours. Burley's a small village and everyone knows everyone else. With one or two notable exceptions.' She gave a nod in the direction of the fields but didn't elaborate.

But Meg followed the direction of the nod, which took her gaze across the gently undulating grassy fields and past the darker verdant woods where now she could make out the red tiled roof of a building. 'What's that place?' she asked.

Tabby hesitated and took a gulp of tea before answering, 'It's Winter Farm. Garth Winter is your nearest neighbour, but you won't see much of him so you needn't worry about being sociable. Anyway, never mind that. Did you notice the way to the village from here? Now, our house is in the second street

9

after the post office . . . '

After Tabby had gone, Katie fell asleep again and the cottage filled with a thick silence, like wadded wool in a box. Meg's uneasiness returned. She went out to the car and got boxes from the boot and back seat, determined to move in properly and find a place for everything. It felt odd, not hearing people and traffic constantly. Even the air tasted different. There was a sweetness to it like mown hay and a sharp tang of salt from the sea, which she knew was not far away, on the other side of the hedgerows and beyond the small village of Burley.

She left the boxes filling the hallway and decided to put Katie to bed first. There were two bedrooms upstairs and Tabby had thoughtfully put fresh linen on both of the beds. Soon Katie was tucked up with Belly Bear, one thumb in her mouth along with the bear's cloth ear. Meg pulled the curtains shut. Then she set herself to the task of sorting her belongings. Most of the furniture and kitchen equipment would follow soon in the removals van. But for now there was a quiet pleasure in folding towels and laying them in the newly discovered airing cupboard and hanging her favourite mug on the mug tree she'd brought with her.

After a hasty dinner of pasta with a jar of ready-made tomato and basil sauce heated and stirred into it, Meg laid out her laptop, paper and pens on the table in the front room. She couldn't afford to have a day off, even today. She worked as a freelance writer and if she didn't work, she didn't get paid. Before marrying Phillip she'd done a variety of jobs in London, including working for a charity and running her own pet-sitting service. Once she'd married, of course, she had given that all up. Now, despite the sometimes long hours she had to put in, there was a satisfaction to working for herself again. She wrote anything and everything from greeting-card messages to articles on housework and being a mum.

Determined not to let the silence get her down, Meg picked up her pen and opened her pad to a fresh blank page. She always wrote her ideas and first drafts longhand and then transferred them to the laptop. She had only written two words when a long shrill alarm made her jump.

'It's the phone, you idiot,' she told herself angrily, willing her heart to stop pounding. She ran out of the room, trying to locate it. The insistent repeated note continued. Like a game of 'hot and cold' she dashed in and out of rooms while the sound got louder or softer. The telephone turned out to be in a tiny cupboard under the stairs, stuffed in at an angle under an old ironing board, a tin of paint and a bag of dog treats. It was an old-fashioned thing, black Bakelite with a ring dial, like something that ought to be in a museum.

Meg grabbed at it and picked up the ancient receiver. 'Hello?'

There was a tinny rush of inter-ference on the line.

'Hello?' she said louder.

There was a click and the line went dead. Shrugging, she untangled the phone and got it out of the cupboard. The ironing board slammed down, its legs caught up in the cord, bruising her shoulder. The tin of paint fell and hit the bag, spilling dried dog biscuits all over the hall floor. The pain made Meg's eyes water and she rubbed her flesh. The tears kept welling up as if all the keyed-up emotions of the day had to burst out of her. Ignoring the crunch of the biscuits under her soles, she half ran to the cottage door and pushed her way out.

She took a deep breath of the evening air and berated herself for being a fool.

'I can do this,' she said out loud. 'I am a grown woman — a mother, for goodness sake. I can do this for me and Katie. This is my new life and it's going to work.' She punched the air with her fists as she spoke.

A man was walking down the lane. He was still far enough away that she couldn't see his features clearly. She got an impression of height, of thick fair hair and lean limbs in faded work trousers and a checked shirt. In embarrassment she lowered her hands, hoping he hadn't heard her shouting to no one. He seemed to sense her watching and looked up then, straight at her. He halted. Meg wondered whether she should wave to him. What would she do if he walked on right to Primrose Cottage? What was the etiquette in the countryside? Perhaps she was meant to invite him in for a cup of tea. All this raced through her mind so that she was relieved and almost disappointed when he abruptly turned on his heel and walked away back up the lane and over the rise.

As she lay in bed that night, unable to sleep in the strange surroundings, the phone began to ring again. She was too bodily tired to get up and go downstairs to answer it. Besides, she was sure it wasn't for her. It had to be for the previous owner of the cottage because no one yet had her new

14

number except Tabby, who preferred to use her mobile and never used land-lines. Certain whoever it was would ring off soon, Meg drifted into a shallow sleep where she was driving along blackened tarmac roads which shifted and changed until she had no idea where she was — only that she wasn't alone on the road; there was someone driving after her. Downstairs on the hall floor, the telephone rang and rang.

# 2

Garth had thought her a girl at first sight. She was so slim and tiny, with long brown hair that rippled onto her shoulders. He had been on his way to Anna's Field to check on the woodlark nest until he realised that someone had moved into Primrose Cottage. He had turned back and although he didn't want to think about her, he wondered why she was crying. If he was a different man, he would have gone to her and asked if she was all right. Instead he'd plodded back up the rise and veered onto the grassy slopes, through the woodland and down the far side to get to the nest. It was a long detour but preferable to meeting her.

He hadn't realised the cottage was sold. It had lain empty for a year since old Vinny Combs died. Her nephew must have managed to sell it after all.

Well, good luck to him. And to her, the young woman who'd taken it on. He was sure he wouldn't see her again. Not now he knew she was there. He had no reason to go in that direction except for the short cut through the gate, and he needn't do that now.

He loved the soft lilac of summer evenings. The smell of the earth rose up to him, warmed by a day's worth of sun: rich Devon clays with a signature perfume all of their own. The birds were beginning to roost for the night — crows gathering at the communal nests, all rustling feathers and muted squawks. The woodlarks were where they were meant to be, on the heathy open grass of Anna's Field. He couldn't see the nest, tucked into the ground as it was, but he knew it was there. When he climbed back up the hill he saw the sea, navy blue, reflecting the coming of the night and the twinkling lights of the village. With a sigh he turned to the farm house. He couldn't put it off any longer. He had to go home.

A scene of devastation met him as soon as he got inside. The easel lay on its side and he saw one leg was broken. The vast canvas was ripped across in a diagonal gape like a wailing mouth. The floor was paint splattered, with oily black and septic green mingling on the tiles. He stared at it without moving. A part of him felt bad about hurling it all to the ground in his rage, but the rest of him was numb. Eventually, he knelt and began to pick up the tubes of oil colours, the splayed brushes and the leaking water cup. He spent a while gluing the easel and carefully splinting its leg. Then he grimly set it upright once more. The canvas he left where it was. It mocked him each time he passed it but he couldn't help it any more than he could help himself.

The next morning, Alex Cranborn arrived, cap in hand and agitated. 'It's them thieves once more, Mr Winter. Gone and tore off the wire netting from the chicken house, they 'ave. Three of 'em took.'

'Call me Garth please, Alex,' Garth said as he had a hundred times before.

Alex was his farm manager and had been for the last four years since Garth had lost his interest in farming and much else in his life. He relied on the man to keep Winter Farm in good shape physically and financially, and so far Alex had done that to his satisfaction.

He stood back to let the other man enter the house. He saw Alex glance at the canvas but he said nothing about it. There was nothing he wanted to say.

'Three chickens stolen, you say?' he asked with an effort. 'Whoever's doing it, it's not large-scale theft.'

'That's true.' Alex inclined his grizzled grey head. 'But it's not right them getting away with it all the same.'

'What's to be done?' But he said it more from a belief that Alex wanted him to respond so, than a real desire for an answer. Like his painting, he'd lost heart in his farm. Inside of him there was a hollow, and it appeared that

19

nothing could fill it; nothing could satisfy it or make him happy.

'I put up new chicken wire and I'm thinking a guard dog'd be the thing.' This last was said with a certain amount of hopeful expectation. Alex knew his feelings about dogs, though not why he disliked them.

'Let's not be hasty,' Garth said. 'Perhaps the stolen chickens'll be the last of it.'

Already his mind was turned elsewhere, thinking he would try again with the paints. At least coat a background on his new canvas upstairs. Let the old one rot.

Alex sniffed loudly and rubbed the drip from his reddened nose. A life of outdoor labour had made a map of his face until it was all folds and veins and wind-burned skin. 'Very well, Mr Winter. We'll leave it at that for now. But I've got a friend whose bitch just pupped. Good guard dogs they'll make. Think on it, will you?'

With a final frown at the canvas lying

in his path on the hallway floor, Alex went out. Garth imagined him shaking his head and complaining to his wife later about the odd Mr Winter up at yonder farm.

He decided he would take the easel and a fresh canvas out into the courtyard at the back of the house. It was sunny and sheltered there and he would have good bright light to work by. It was both a curse and a blessing not to have to work for a living, he mused as he rummaged in the upstairs room for new brushes. His father had made an excellent business of running Winter Farm and had passed it on to his only son in very good shape. Garth, in his turn, had worked hard and passionately at farming the land that had been in the Winter family's ownership for centuries. They were bred into the very landscape, as his father liked to say. When Garth married Anna, he knew they would have their happy-ever-after right here on the precious Devon soil of his farm and bring up a clatter of boys, one of whom was destined to inherit the farmhouse and the vast acreage of fields and copses that went with it.

He paused in the process of choosing a canvas and laughed harshly. What an arrogant fool he'd been, thinking he could choose his own future. Now he lived alone, rattling around like a pea in a tin can in the huge house, the fields at first rampant with burdock and thistle and the blown seeds of willow herb until Alex Cranborn had arrived, offering him a deal he couldn't refuse. In a sense, Alex had saved his life with his offer to run the farm for him as manager. At any point he could take over again, but that point had not yet arrived. Maybe it never would.

There was a song in the air. Garth let go of the canvas and went to the window to squint down. He hadn't imagined it. There was a small child in his courtyard. It was wearing a pink summer dress and was hunkered down, drawing on his slabs with blue chalk. At least he hoped it was chalk and not crayon, which wouldn't come off. He lifted a bunched hand to rap his knuckles on the dusty pane but stopped. Instead, not wanting to startle the child, he went down and out the back door into the sunshine.

'What are you doing here?' His voice came out more sternly than he meant.

The little girl gave a start but didn't seem scared. She waved the stubby chalk at him. 'Look, I can draw a flower.'

He saw she had indeed drawn a flower. Right on his patio. In fact, several flowers, all blue with four petals and a smiley face in the middle.

'You're trespassing,' he said abruptly. Where had she come from? Was she one of Tabby Shaw's brood? He couldn't remember how many offspring she had but he was aware that she had been housekeeper while Primrose Cottage remained empty. Vinny's nephew lived in London and never made it south to check on it.

'I'm Katie,' she said, not bothering to listen to his big, long word. 'Do you like drawing flowers?'

He saw he was still holding a paint brush, which she was pointing to. 'Look kid,' he said, 'I'm not very sociable, so you can't stay here. You understand?'

*   *   *

Meg was frantic. Katie was gone. She'd been playing in the garden at the back of the cottage and Meg was so busy she hadn't checked on her for an hour. There was nowhere to go to apart from the fields, and she'd specifically told Katie to stay close and not go out the back gate. Katie was scared of the sheep in the fields and nodded. Meg couldn't understand where or why she'd gone.

Tabby had phoned while Meg was clearing up the dog treats after preparing breakfast for Katie. After shovelling the cereal down, Katie had then gone into the garden to play, taking her plastic bucket of chalks with her. Meg left the back door open so she could see her.

'Hey, how's it going? Did you sleep well?' Tabby's cheerful voice filled her ear.

'Yes, thanks,' Meg lied. Her sleep had been shallow and ridden with night-mares. Waking to the sheep lowing and some kind of insect battering against the glass of her bedroom window had unsettled her further. Usually the seven o'clock bus which stopped right outside their flat in London woke her up with its early commuters and their loud chat as they got on board. 'Listen Tabby, did you phone me last night?'

'Phone you? No, I didn't. I reckoned you'd both get an early night after your journey. Besides, my phone was out of charge last night. Silly me, I'm always forgetting to charge it up.'

'No, this was on the landline. Never mind. It probably was a wrong number or a sales pitch.'

'Or a friend to wish you luck in your new home?'

Meg sensed Tabby fishing for information. She knew very little about Meg's married life in London. She couldn't know that there were no friends to wish her luck.

'Perhaps,' she said noncommittally, then changing the subject swiftly, 'When's Ellen's party starting?'

'Oh goodness, you've reminded me of all the stuff I've still got to prepare. It's at two, and the kids are all desperate to meet Katie of course, and it'll be lovely for you and Maurice to see each other again after all this time. It's going to be mayhem — I think Ellen's invited her whole class. But we can sit and drink wine to numb the pain. Must go; see you later!'

Meg smiled as she tucked her mobile into her pocket. Tabby was full of energy and positive about life. She was just what Meg needed. She felt lighter and more positive herself this morning. It was another beautiful day and she was free of the past. Just as she reassured herself of that, she realised she couldn't hear Katie out in the back and with a whoosh, all her fears rushed back in like the sea on dry sand.

'Katie?' she called as she ran out into the back garden.

It was a pretty place with a small patio edged with borders of periwinkle, lupins, pinks and other colourful flowers she didn't know the names of. But there was no Katie. Meg shaded her eyes and scanned the surroundings. The fields were bare of anything but grass and sheep. Where could she be? Her heart was painful in her chest and her breath grew short.

*Calm it,* she thought. *It's not London. She's simply wandered off. But where?*

She saw the red roof tiles on the crest of the slope flashing in the sunlight. What had Tabby called it? Winter Farm, that was it. It was the only other building nearby. She tried to think whether Katie's little legs could take her that far. Meg slipped her sandals onto her bare feet and ran out through the garden gate.

She was wary of the sheep as she hurried over the tussocky grass towards the farm. It was a relief to discover that they were more frightened of her, moving clumsily away as she forged on. She reached the farmhouse only slightly out of breath after the run up the gradient. It was a lovely old house, built of red brick and weathered beams and a thick, dark green ivy ran up and over the doorway, lazily woven with cream petals and fat bumblebees. At either side of the front step was a small stone lion, but they too were weathered and one had lost part of its stone face, so it looked scarred and sad.

She paused, finger ready to press the bell. She wasn't ready to meet her neighbours, really, but what choice did she have? She pushed the bell down firmly. There was no response. After three attempts she gave up and stood for a moment undecided. Then sheer, desperate longing for Katie made her turn and walk down the side of the farm house to its back grounds. She didn't entertain the notion that her daughter wasn't here. There were too many wild places a child could fall into and not be readily found.

A man was sitting on a wicker chair on a wide patio. The first thing she noticed about him was his eyes. They were unusually dark blue, like seawater at night, and there seemed a vulnerability in them which was at odds with the rest of his stance. It was the man she'd seen walking towards them on the lane the evening before. His fair hair was thick and tousled as if he hadn't bothered to brush it, and there was a day's set of bristles on his firm jaw. When he saw her he stiffened, and his face looked positively unwelcoming. He rose from the chair and seemed to tower over her.

But that didn't matter, because behind him she saw Katie crouched over a piece of paper, painting gaudy red from a small pot. The relief hit her with the power of a tsunami. Meg ran past the man and gathered her daughter in a fierce hug.

'Katie, Katie, what are you doing? I told you to stay in the garden. That was so, so naughty of you.' But she kept kissing her and hugging her so the reprimand was useless.

Katie struggled in her grasp and pushed to be let down. 'I'm painting. Look, Mummy, it's bedtime for the sun. Garth gave me a brush.' She showed a paintbrush, its hairs spread with paint as if an electric shock had gone into it.

Meg was suddenly conscious of the man. She felt embarrassed at bursting into his garden, and then angry at him for letting her daughter be there when she had imagined the worst.

'How could you?' she said. 'I was so worried. I . . . ' She couldn't explain her turmoil. In horror she felt tears prick her eyes.

'She was safe here,' he said. 'If you hadn't come then I'd have arranged for Mrs Shaw to pick her up.' His voice was low and pleasant, with a faint burr of Devonshire warming a cultured English accent. It made her think of melting honey.

'All the same,' she said disapprovingly. She couldn't think what to add to that. Katie was safe, that was what mattered. Now she just wanted to leave. She had no desire to socialise, no energy for the niceties that went with it. Primrose Cottage suddenly seemed like a refuge, and her urge was to grab her daughter and run to it.

He stiffened and his face was closed, with no smile or warmth to soften his expression. He'd picked up then on her anger — her dislike of him, if that was what it was.

'I'm a quiet man. I don't like visitors. I don't encourage them.'

'That suits me very well,' she snapped back, thinking him unutterably rude, although he'd simply voiced what she felt too. 'I'll take my daughter and go. I'm your new neighbour, Meg Lyons, but we don't need to meet again.'

'That suits me too,' he replied in a terse voice.

'But Mummy, I haven't finished my picture,' Katie wailed as Meg took her hand and pulled her up. 'Garth said I can use the red paint.'

'I'll carry your paper,' Meg said. 'Leave the paintbrush and the paint; they're not yours.'

She felt the heat rise in her face as Katie bawled noisily and she dragged her down the side of the farmhouse and out onto the lane. She felt indignantly angry at Garth Winter. He was rude and unfriendly and unhelpful, and she didn't care if she never saw him again.

\* \* \*

'Rude, unfriendly and unhelpful? That doesn't sound like Garth Winter,' Tabby said, looking at her sharply when she regaled her friend with the morning's events later that day.

Ellen's party was in full swing. The Shaws had a large, sprawling garden which was mostly lawn. Maurice had set up a bouncy castle on the grass and a paddling pool. Ten girls were running about in their swimsuits, screaming and splashing and eating ice-creams. The noise level was incredible. Ellen's brothers had vanished to play over at friends' homes and Jane and Katie were sitting together on the double swings, smeared in chocolate ices and kicking their feet happily.

Tabby and Meg were in the bright, airy kitchen where they could look out at the children while they prepared the party tea. The door was open wide, letting in the happy sounds, the sweet, hot air and the occasional confused bee. Meg chopped orange segments and apple slices for the fruit salad. Tabby frowned at the raspberry jellies, which hadn't set properly. She carried them back to the fridge, still talking over her shoulder.

'He keeps himself to himself but he was helpful when the storms blew the roof tiles off the cottage a couple of winters ago. Lent me his farmhands to fix it all. He's pleasant enough when I occasionally see him over there. You know, I've been caring for Primrose for Vinny's family until they could sell it. And you say he was rude? Well I never.'

Meg flushed and concentrated on cutting precise blocks of fruit. She thought of the paintbrush cast aside on the slabs where she'd made Katie drop it and the little paint pot with its lid off, crimson drops sliding down its side. With a pang of guilt, she had to admit he had been very kind to Katie. In her fear and anxiety she hadn't acted well. It was just as well they'd both sworn to stay away from each other.

'Is he an artist?' she asked. There had been an easel on Garth Winter's patio and a blank canvas propped on it.

Tabby nodded. 'He's a good one, too, from all accounts. Gilda Mable down on Stockey Road in the village is his agent. She takes the paintings to London and sells them for him at a gallery.'

'Doesn't he go himself?' Meg asked.

Tabby sighed and shook her head. 'It's a sad story, but you'll hear it soon enough in the village so I'm not telling you anything that's a secret. He and his wife were in a car crash about four years ago. She died and he came out of it unscathed. It was very shocking for everyone but there were mutterings amongst some about how come he had no injuries, apart from minor ones, while Anna was killed.'

'But that's daft,' Meg said indignantly. 'These things are simply the luck of the draw. It wasn't his fault.'

'I agree with you, but the rumours persisted. In the end Garth holed up at Winter Farm and became something of a recluse. Alex Cranborn runs his farm for him and Gilda sells his art. He must order his food and supplies online because I've never seen him set foot in Burley in the last four years.'

'How sad,' Meg said, and felt it too. But she wouldn't dwell on it. There was no reason to. Winter Farm was out of bounds and she'd tell Katie that firmly. She finished pouring the sweetened orange juice over the fruit in the bowl and gave it to Tabby for chilling. But every so often that afternoon she found herself thinking about Garth Winter and the appeal in his midnight blue eyes which he imagined hidden from the world.

* * *

Katie was hot and cranky when they got back to the cottage. It was after six o'clock. They'd both caught the sun, Meg realised, looking at Katie's pink cheeks and new freckles. Her own face was browned, she saw, glancing in the hall mirror. She tanned easily. The woman in the mirror looked relaxed and sun-kissed with her brown hair flecked with copper. She'd done the right thing, bringing them here.

She managed to get Katie into her night dress and helped her brush her teeth. The little girl fell asleep instantly, cuddled with Belly Bear, her head cradled by the soft pillow. Meg stood looking down at her and felt that ever-surprising rush of love flooding her. She'd do anything to protect Katie and to keep her happy. Phillip didn't know what he was missing. How could a father reject his only child? The unspoken question left a sour taste in her mouth. She kissed Katie's head gently and tiptoed out.

Coming down the stairs quietly, intending to go into the kitchen and make a cup of tea, Meg saw a slim package half tucked under the front doormat. The post had been delivered during the day while they were out and she hadn't noticed it on their arrival back.

She picked it up curiously. There was no one she imagined who would send her something. Her parents were long dead and she had no brothers or sisters. Any friends she'd had were distant now, thanks to Phillip.

It was a yellow A5 padded envelope, the sort you might send a book in. The label on the front was typed so there were no clues there. She slit it open and felt inside. But it was empty. Frowning in puzzlement, she shook it, then turned it over. There was another sticky label on the back, long and thin. On it was her Tottenham address.

# 3

She woke drenched in sweat. There was
a tapping at the window and her heart
clenched painfully. She staggered from
bed and flung back the curtain. A small
bird flew off. Meg tried to breathe. In
and out. In and out. That was the way.
But the envelope was still there. She
had placed it on her bedside cabinet. It
wasn't a dream. It was very real. She
ran her fingers over it once more.

'Mummy,' Katie wailed.

Meg ran into the other bedroom but
Katie was all right. She stretched out
her arms to Meg.

'Where's Belly Bear? He's not here.'

Meg retrieved the bear from the floor
and handed it over. She needed to get
a grip. The cottage was secure. She'd
gone round last night checking windows and making sure the doors were
locked. It reminded her of Tottenham,

where every time she went out to the shops she had the same routine.

After a hot shower, breakfast and coffee she felt normal. She decided to go and see Tabby. She'd make up for it by working late that evening. She popped a protesting Katie into her buggy and set off for the village. The lane was closed in by high Devon banks and thick hedgerows. If anyone came down the lane she'd be trapped in a tunnel of hawthorn, dog rose and honeysuckle. For a moment she thought of Winter Farm, out of sight but just up there on the left behind the rise of the hill. It was reassuring. But then she remembered Garth Winter's terse comments about visitors and her own snappy response. He wouldn't welcome her.

'You must've smelt the coffee,' Tabby greeted her cheerfully. 'Come along in. Jane's building a lovely muddy sandcastle in the paddling pool and I'm sure she'd love Katie to help her.'

Meg sank gratefully onto one of Tabby's brightly painted kitchen chairs and felt a wave of comfortable ease wash over her. This was a place where nothing awful could happen. A door slammed somewhere and she shot upright, heart thudding.

'It's just the kids. The joy of the school holidays, having them about all day.' Tabby looked at her strangely. 'Are you okay? You seem rather jumpy.' She pushed a large mug of coffee in front of Meg.

Meg pulled the envelope from her bag and set it carefully on Tabby's kitchen table. Her throat constricted. She couldn't explain it.

Tabby picked it up with a frown and shook it to free its contents. 'What's all this about? Why have you brought me an empty envelope?'

'It came in the post yesterday,' Meg said. 'Sent from my address in Tottenham.'

'And? I don't understand.' Tabby took a sip of her coffee. In the garden there was shrieking and happy giggling.

'Neither do I. But I think Phillip sent it.'

There was a moment of silence while Tabby digested this. Then she stared at Meg. 'You've never really told me about what happened between you and Phillip.' Her tone was gentle.

'I . . . I couldn't, somehow,' Meg said, willing herself not to cry. For goodness sake, what was wrong with her? She was so edgy, and there were enough tears in reserve to fill a lake if she let them fall. 'My wedding was so perfect, wasn't it?' she added wistfully.

'Yes, it was lovely. I remember thinking that Phillip must be incredibly wealthy. It was wonderfully extravagant.' Tabby smiled. 'And he was the most handsome man I'd ever seen — like a movie star. You were gorgeous, too, in that beautiful wedding dress and with the orange blossom spray. So romantic.'

'That's what I mean,' Meg said. She rubbed her nose.

Tabby pushed a box of paper tissues across the table and Meg took one.

'And you were so awfully busy after

the honeymoon that I never quite caught up with you,' Tabby said. 'You had Katie pretty quickly and then I only saw her once, at the baby shower.' There was no bitterness in Tabby's voice, Meg noted with relief, but a puzzlement.

'Phillip insisted on the baby shower to show Katie off,' Meg said wryly. 'He wanted to present his perfect family to the world.'

'And it wasn't perfect?' Tabby guessed. She poured more coffee and touched Meg's hand sympathetically.

'Anything but perfect. Almost immediately after we got married, he changed. He liked to be in control, and I . . . well at first I liked it. That sounds bad but I wanted to be his wife, the love of his life, and if that meant bending to his will, then I wanted to do it. But it got to the stage where he was telling me what to wear and who I could see and gradually I wasn't allowed to see my friends. But it was very subtle and I didn't realise it until I had no one left.'

43

'I had no idea.' Tabby sounded appalled. 'I should've done more. I should've demanded we meet.'

Meg shook her head. 'You weren't to know. I became very good at giving excuses to people. I was too busy or the baby was sick or we were going away at the weekend. There was a string of reasons to put friends off.'

'But you had the strength to leave him in the end. You went to Tottenham,' Tabby prompted.

'It wasn't strength, it was fear,' Meg said starkly. Her hand shook slightly as she reached for her mug. She waited until it stilled. She had to be strong now. She'd been running in fear for so long, and now she'd changed her life and Katie's life. This was their new beginning.

'He became very moody, and when he was in a dark mood he could be very threatening. He never hit me, but I always felt there was a possibility that he could. One evening it was very bad. I was terrified for myself and for the

44

baby. So I waited until the next day when he went to work, and I left.'

'Did he find you?'

'That's the thing. I thought we were hidden. The divorce was arranged through the lawyers so there was no reason for him to be given my address. He married again quite quickly and I was very relieved. I thought I was off the hook.'

Tabby picked up the envelope and stared at it. 'But why would he send you this now? And how did he know where to send it?'

Meg stood up and walked to the window. Out on the sunny lawn the two little girls were crouched in the empty paddling pool with buckets and spades and a pile of golden sand. She sighed.

'About a year ago I began to feel as if someone was watching the flat. There was nothing I could put my finger on, but it became very uncomfortable. I was convinced that Phillip had found me. Then my inheritance came through and that was when I knew I could leave

45

London and make a new life here.'

'So you never actually saw Phillip in Tottenham?' Tabby asked slowly.

'No,' Meg said. 'Look, I'm sorry I didn't get in touch with you until I needed to move. I was ashamed of where we were living. Ashamed at where I'd ended up after my perfect wedding.'

Tabby held the envelope out to her. 'Don't you think it might simply have been forwarded by the post office? Some old aunt or other ancient relative wanting to send you something but who's forgotten to enclose the item?'

Meg's shoulders went down. 'Maybe you're right. I was left that money by an old aunt. Perhaps it's from her estate and the lawyers sent it on.'

'It's unlikely that Phillip would hunt you down in Tottenham, isn't it? Didn't you say he'd remarried?'

'Yes, to a Leila Graham. You've probably seen her in the gossip mags. She's from a shipping family.'

'Well then,' Tabby said with a satisfied grin, 'no offence, darling girl, but why would Phillip be following you when he's got a lovely heiress to be photographed with? Now come along and help me mix a cake for lunch. You worry too much, that's your problem. You should relax more. Now, here's the mixing bowl and a wooden spoon. You can be the cook.'

Meg did feel more relaxed as she helped Tabby prepare a lunch which looked like it might feed five thousand. Apparently Jacob and William had friends coming over and Ellen's two best friends were invited too. Then there were Meg and Katie, who simply must stay to help eat the cake, as well as Tabby herself. What a pity Maurice was working and would miss out.

The air of normality in the Shaw household made Meg admit to herself that she was getting things out of all proportion. Tabby was right. She'd never actually seen Phillip in Tottenham. Although once on the High Street she thought she had. There had been a tall man who walked like him. She'd run to catch him up but he vanished into the busy crowds. Then there had been the odd telephone call over the two years: calls that when she picked them up there was nothing but rushing air on the other end, and maybe someone listening and breathing while she asked who was there.

She walked home alone after the lunch. Jane had asked if Katie could stay for a sleepover and Tabby had persuaded her that the kids would be fine. They were going to play indoors with Lego bricks and colouring books as the weather had cooled and the sun was shaded under thickening grey clouds. Now there was a mist of rain over the hillside and she shivered in her thin cotton summer dress. Strange how quickly one could get used to proper summer weather. She hugged her arms around herself and wished for a jacket.

The walk took her through the village, two streets along from Tabby's house and then past the post office which doubled as the village store.

There were plenty of people out and about, and tourists too, as Burley was a popular, quaint Devon village with thatched cottages and narrow streets and ever-busy beaches. Once Meg left the village it got quieter immediately. There was a footpath which led a little way and avoided the traffic, but the final stretch was back onto the isolated hedged lane ending at the rusted gate and Primrose Cottage.

Suddenly Meg didn't want to go that way. She came to the end of the little footpath and hesitated. To the left was the road that led in the direction of Torquay and from it, the lane forked off toward the cottage. To the right, the road headed eventually to Lyme Regis. Then she noticed an overgrown path cutting into the bank on the other side of the road. It looked like it was going in roughly the right direction to lead her back home, if she didn't mind walking over the fields. She waited until there was a gap in the cars whizzing past and ran across. Her feet were slippery in her damp sandals and now her legs were wet from the sodden grasses. Tiny grass flower heads stuck to her skin as she brushed past them. The hem of her dress was darkened with water from the wayside plants. She slipped through the gap in the hedge and was into the fields.

She almost didn't mind the sheep now. She smiled to herself. For a city girl she wasn't doing too badly. As if to remind her that she was in the midst of nature, the rain sharpened and a heavy shower pelted down on her. Meg shrieked. The water was cold and hard on her scalp, and her wet hair slapped her cheeks as she half ran towards the far stone wall that split the fields. She scrambled over a stile and with relief saw two buildings not far away. They were made of grey stone and red, corrugated tin roofs. Beyond, in the near distance, she saw Winter Farm. The cottage wasn't far away then. Meg decided she'd take shelter in one of the barns until the rain subsided.

She reached the nearest barn and pushed at the door. Thankfully it opened with a wooden creak and she almost fell inside. The air was dusty and there was the hulk of a big tractor and a pool of ill-smelling black oil on the ground. Bales of hay were stacked to the roof and she sneezed twice. Drops of cold rain trickled down her back, and then she was shivering and sneezing and wishing she was back in the civilized city.

She stood against the tractor and listened to the thud of the raindrops on the tin roof. Once it lightened she'd make for the cottage, she decided. Behind her, in the hay bales, came a rustling sound. Meg froze. There it was again. All her fears about Phillip came flooding back. Was he here? Had he followed her somehow from Tottenham to Devon? Why was he doing this?

Whatever it was, it was bigger than a mouse. Heaven forbid it could be rats. Meg swallowed. She crept round the side of the tractor, then she paused.

This was ridiculous. Why would Phillip be hiding in Garth Winter's farm? Her imagination was getting out of hand. She stood upright, determined to be sensible. A figure slipped from the shadows and out of the door. Meg screamed then ran after it. She tripped on the bottom of the door and stumbled out into the open. There was no one there. But there was another barn.

Meg hammered on the front door of Winter Farm. She didn't care whether Garth Winter liked visitors or not. The door opened and he stared at her. She tried to ignore how blue his eyes were.

'There's a man in your barn. You've got to do something,' she cried.

He didn't try to argue with her or waste time asking her to repeat her statement, but calmly shut the door behind him and followed her up over the fields to the barns. Meg stood and pointed to the first barn.

'He's in there.'

Garth Winter glanced at her and she nodded slightly. She was aware of his height and the strong breadth of his shoulders. This wasn't a man who would be easily intimidated by whoever was in the barn. She felt a warm surge of confidence now he was there. He opened the barn door and went in. Meg waited. The rain had stopped and the sun was shining now. There was steam rising from her sodden dress. She smelt the scent of her shampoo from her wet hair. A bird sang, spiralling up over the red barn roof until it was a speck in the bright sky. He came back out of the barn slowly.

'Well?' Meg demanded.

He shook his head. 'There's no one there.'

'But I saw him. He was in the other barn when I went in there to shelter from the rain. He must've seen me and escaped into this barn. He must be in there.' Meg ran forward into the building.

This barn was empty except for an old car half draped in tarpaulin, and barrels of animal feed. There was nowhere for someone to hide. Embarrassed, she went out again. She had imagined the whole thing. That was the only explanation. She'd allowed her fears about her ex-husband to colour reality. It had to stop. She had her new life. Now she had to live it.

'I'm sorry,' Meg said, tilting her head up so that she could look him in the eye.

'There's no harm done,' Garth said.

She was surprised. Wasn't he angry with her for disturbing him? This man who didn't like visitors?

'Would you like a towel? You're soaked,' he said.

Now there was stiff politeness in his voice. He didn't want her to bother him further. Well, she didn't want to be there either. Meg was suddenly conscious of how she looked. She was bedraggled and muddy and her hair was flattened to her head. She flushed as she realised her dress was clinging damply to her curves. Still, he didn't seem to have noticed that.

'No thank you. I'm nearly home.'

With her head held high, Meg started to walk confidently down the slope. A tussock grabbed her ankle and she stumbled. He set her upright as she leaned unexpectedly into him.

'Sorry,' she mumbled. His touch had awakened her nerves and a fire shot through her where their skin had met. What was that about? She didn't like him. He was a boor. So what if he had the darkest blue eyes she'd ever seen. They were wasted on him.

'Goodbye Mrs Lyons.' His tone was curt and unfriendly, just as it had been the previous day.

'Goodbye Mr Winter,' she returned, equally abruptly.

She stalked off down the slope, not caring if he was following. When she got to the garden gate she looked back. She couldn't see him of course, only the roof of the farm house. His touch lingered on her skin.

# 4

Garth checked on the chicken shed. It wasn't his job anymore. Alex Cranborn did that along with the running of the rest of the farm. But it had turned into a pleasant, softly warm evening after the heavy showers of the afternoon and Garth was strangely restless. Alex was finished for the day so there was no worry about bumping into him and having to exchange conversation about the farm. The farmhands likewise had gone home. Garth's house was silent, the way he liked it, but he found himself outside, striding across the bumps and familiar hollows of his land. The shapely outline of her body flashed again into his mind. She hadn't noticed how her damp dress clung to her in all the right places. His body had stirred, like a machine never used suddenly springing into life. It was wrong of him.

*Mrs Lyons*. She was married. So where was her husband? Why was she so scared? And had she honestly seen someone in his barn?

The chicken house was securely fastened. Alex Cranborn was meticulous, Garth knew that. He didn't actually have to check on the chickens; he had to get Meg Lyons out of his head. She wasn't the slip of a girl that she looked. Although she was small and slender, she was, on closer view, very much a woman. She had high cheekbones, a full mouth and eyes the colour of storm clouds. She was a very attractive woman, and he shouldn't be thinking about her. Garth stopped stock still. He sighed and ran his fingers through his hair in exasperation at himself. He was in an odd mood, that was certain. He looked back at Winter Farm. It was his place of safety, yet he was reluctant to go back to it tonight. From his vantage point high up on the crest of the low hill, he could see beyond his red tiled roof to the dark brown thatch of Primrose Cottage.

He hoped she had calmed from her distress that afternoon. He didn't like to think of her and the little girl scared. There was nothing to fear. He took a deep breath of the sweet evening air. There was no place on earth as beautiful as this Devon land. It was soft and undulating and rich in nature. He decided he'd walk as far as the long fields. There was no harm in double-checking the barns, and it gave him an extension to his wanderings. After that he'd go home, make a strong coffee and do a little sketching.

Dusk was filtering through the sky as he reached the barns, and the old stones were soaked in the lilac light. He went into the first barn, steeling himself as ever for the sight of the car. He forced himself to pull back the tarpaulin, like ripping open a slowly healing wound. The part of the car that had been hidden from sight was gouged and bent. The front fender was crunched like a paper tissue. He looked at it, then he threw the tarp back over the car. He then went quickly over to the other barn.

He sensed another's presence immediately. There was nothing out of the ordinary to be seen, but his sixth sense knew he wasn't alone. He scanned the big tractor and the stacked bales. He wondered whether he should've brought his shotgun, but he was unafraid. He was bigger than most men and likely to win in any fight. He hoped it wouldn't come to that. He wasn't a man to go looking for trouble, but he'd discovered that trouble could find him.

'Come out now,' he said quietly.

There was no sound except for a gentle whistle of breeze past the wooden door. The wind was getting up. Garth sighed. He was ready for his chair and his solitude in the house now.

'Let's hurry this up,' he said louder, standing loose-limbed and at ease. 'Show yourself. If not, then I'll have to get the police out and that's going to mess up everyone's evening.'

There was a rustling in the hay and he tensed, ready. A figure unfolded itself from the shadows and stood in front of the bales. He guessed it was preparing for flight, but he'd get to the door first if it came to it.

'Who are you?' he asked calmly.

He stepped forward. The figure froze. Now Garth saw the intruder that had so terrified Meg. It was a skinny youth with hunched shoulders, clad only in dirty jeans, a thin T-shirt and muddy sneakers. The boy's dark hair was greasy, as if he hadn't washed it in a very long time. He held an equally grimy kit bag.

'What are you doing in my barn?' Garth asked curiously.

He was careful not to sound annoyed. The boy shifted from one foot to the other nervously. 'I was only passing by, honest.'

'What's your name?'

The boy hesitated. 'Ben,' he said.

'And how old are you, Ben?' Garth said, judging him to be no more than sixteen.

'I'm eighteen, sir.'

Garth decided not to argue with him. 'I suppose you're the culprit that took my chickens.' He put a hand up as the boy mumbled something and looked ashamed. 'We won't worry about that now. Are you hungry?'

*　*　*

Garth cooked up fried eggs and bacon and set them down in front of his guest with a plate of toast. Ben didn't wait but took up his knife and fork eagerly and crammed the food into his mouth. Garth poured two mugs of coffee and pushed one across. The boy took a break from eating to gulp the hot liquid, coughing on it.

'Easy,' Garth said. 'Slow it down. There's no hurry.'

When he'd drunk his own coffee, he left the boy mopping up the yellow of the egg with a piece of toast, and went to find his sketch pad. He'd give his visitor a moment to adjust to a full stomach before he decided what to do with him.

Garth smiled wryly. For a man who didn't welcome visitors, he seemed to attract them like a magnet. First the little girl, Katie Lyons, then her mother, and now this stray youth.

'I didn't eat your chickens,' Ben said. He stood in the doorway of Garth's study, hands stuck in pockets and giving off an air of uncertainty.

'What did you do with them?'

'I was going to take them and sell them. But then when I caught one, I couldn't bring myself to try to harm it. While I was thinking on what to do, three of them ran out under the wire. I think a fox got them. I saw one hanging around. I . . . I'm sorry.'

Garth smiled. Not a bad youth then. Just a boy who shouldn't be wandering around strange farms on his own.

Ben winced.

'Have you hurt yourself?'

'It's nothing. I scraped against the tractor when I was trying to get away from the lady earlier.'

Garth demanded to see the boy's leg.

The dirty denim was rolled up to reveal a shallow gash, half congealed.

'That looks nasty. It needs antiseptic and a bandage.' He didn't have these items in the house. To have them required an element of caring for himself and an interest in the minutiae of life. Neither of these he had.

*　*　*

It took longer than expected for her to answer his knock at the cottage. Then he heard the click and rattle of locks before she opened the door. He raised an eyebrow. Out in the country it was unusual to lock up on more than a snib's worth of security. Meg stared up at him. No smile. He wasn't surprised. They had parted earlier in a frosty way. It was mostly his fault. He hadn't wanted that sharp pull of desire for her. He'd offered her a chance to dry off after the heavy showers, but he hadn't meant it, and she had seen right through him. He hadn't wanted her to come

63

back with him to the farm; hadn't wanted the *involvement* required with another human being. Especially this woman, who had an unsettling effect on him.

'This is Ben. He's hurt his leg. Wondered if you had any salve.' He mentally kicked himself. He could hardly string a pleasant sentence together for her. Living alone, he didn't need to chat much. Alex wasn't a conversationalist. Talking was a skill that dried up if left unused.

'How bad is your leg?' Meg asked the boy.

He shrugged in the laid-back teenager way. Meg gestured them inside. Garth ducked in under the lintel. The cottage was scented of a mixture of lavender and thyme and tomato sauce. There was a vase of purple sprigs in the tiny hallway. The tomato aroma was from her dinner.

'Are we disturbing your meal?' he asked.

'No, no, it's fine. I'm finished. Won't you take a seat while I look at Ben's leg?'

So that was how it was to be. She was

formally polite with him. She might never have arrived flushed and soaked at his house, looking for help. He sat where indicated, on a chair in her cosy kitchen. There was a dish with the remains of a pasta meal and an empty wine glass. She saw him looking and took the plate and glass away to the sink. Was she as uncomfortable with him as he was with her?

He watched as she poured warm water and fetched a cloth and a bottle of antiseptic liquid. She chatted easily with Ben, gradually drawing him out with casual questions as she cleaned his wound. So it was only Garth she couldn't talk to. When the leg was bandaged, she took the boy through to her living room and he heard the low sound of the television and Meg's voice murmuring and Ben's answer.

Meg came back and sat opposite him at the table. There was a moment of silence between them. In it he saw how flawless her skin was, and the tiny lines radiating from the corners of her eyes.

They added character to her loveliness. A sign that she'd laughed, somewhere in the past.

'Is he a relative of yours?' Meg asked.

'What?' He was taken aback. 'No, he's your intruder in the barn. A runaway, I guess.'

A long sigh escaped her lips and the tenseness he sensed bristling around her vanished. He didn't imagine it. She had been scared that afternoon. Whatever it was that scared her, it wasn't a random fear of strangers lurking. If it wasn't Ben she was afraid of, then who was it? Then Garth was irked. He didn't want to get involved with her problems. With her. Or with anyone. He should go. But she was speaking.

'Ben should rest for a while; he's exhausted. Would you like a drink?'

'A coffee, thank you,' he found himself replying.

It gave him an opportunity to study her as she boiled the kettle and stood on tiptoe to reach for the coffee jar in a cupboard. There was a vulnerability to her despite her beauty. Everything about her was understated. Most attractive women, in his experience, dressed up to it and elaborated on what nature had given them. But Meg was wearing soft brushed jeans and a faded blue blouse. Her hair hung glossy but unstyled. She wore no makeup. He liked her look. More than liked. He should leave. But now she laid the coffee in front of him and added a jug of cream and a bowl of sugar to the table.

'Vinny's cottage is looking nice,' Garth said, filling the air between them. Anything to distract him from the impulse to reach over to her and tuck that strand of hair behind her ear.

'Thanks, I feel I've moved in properly now. The removals van arrived this afternoon with my few pieces of furniture, so now they're in place that's me ready.'

'I shouldn't call it Vinny's cottage anymore,' he said. 'It looks very different.'

'Are you sorry about that?' Meg smiled and propped her chin on her hands.

'Not at all. Poor old Vinny couldn't

cope by the end and the nephew didn't make any effort. His visits from London were fleeting. He had no feel for the country.'

'I have a little sympathy for that,' Meg laughed, 'I felt a bit scared, too, the day we arrived down from the city. I find it very quiet after city streets, and I'm gradually getting used to the sheep in the field.'

'So you're from London too. I didn't realise. Your accent doesn't show it.'

'I'm from the north originally, but I lived and worked in London for many years. When I got married, I thought I'd be there for the rest of my life.'

They both stopped talking: Garth, because he realised he was learning too much about her; and Meg, from the expression on her face, because she felt she'd given too much away.

'Will your husband be joining you soon?' Why on earth had that come out? He's spoken what was in his mind without filtering it. Now she'd think him intrusive.

She flushed, making him even more uncomfortable. 'No, he won't be coming here. He's my ex-husband actually. Primrose Cottage is for me and Katie.'

'I'm sorry, I shouldn't have asked. It's none of my business.' Garth stood up. 'I'll take the boy back up to the farm.'

'What will you do with him? He looks a sight younger than the eighteen he says he is. Shouldn't we let the police know?' She sounded relieved, too, at the change in conversation. They could both concentrate on the safe topic of the runaway.

'He'd only run off. I can't stop him if he wants to do that. I'll let him stay a few days and then we'll see.'

The decision was made then. Until he told Meg, he hadn't been sure what to do with the boy. He couldn't just turn him out. Winter Farm was large enough that they didn't need to interact much. He'd give Ben one of the bedrooms in the top of the house. He'd have his privacy and Garth would have his. After that, well they'd turn that corner when it came.

He turned to go to the living room. Meg caught his arm. It startled him. He felt the imprint of her fingertips gently pressing into his skin. Then it was gone, so quickly he thought he'd imagined it.

'I wanted to apologise for my behaviour yesterday, when Katie was lost. I was unforgivably rude to you.'

He suddenly *liked* her. It was separate from the attraction he had for her, unwanted but stubbornly present. Not many people, in his experience, were able to say sorry, to admit a fault. 'Nothing to apologise for,' he said gruffly. 'You were worried about your daughter. If I'd known she was yours, I'd have brought her down to the cottage.'

Ben was stretched out on the sofa, covered by a pink patchwork quilt and watching a kids' TV channel more suited to pre-schoolers. Garth glanced at Meg and they exchanged a smile. He looked so young, and nothing like the lurking figure in the barn that had caused so much panic.

* * *

Back at Winter Farm, Garth aired the back bedroom while Ben hovered in the background. He searched for some of his old clothes to give the boy. The wardrobe was a big ancient oak affair, voluminous and dark. As he brushed aside hanging coats, they released old scent. Anna's perfume. A lilac silk dress slithered from a hanger, disturbed by his foraging. A deep pang of regret hit him, as deep as an ocean of tears: for the past, and for the way things had ended between them.

He grabbed an old shirt and trousers and shut the wardrobe. But he couldn't shut the door to the past in his mind so easily. He left Ben crashed out and snoring on the bed and went to the sanctuary of his study downstairs. What had he done, letting the boy stay here?

It was a breach in his defences, however tiny. After the accident, he'd sworn to keep people at bay. Winter Farm was his place of safety. He'd learned that it was better to be alone. Anna had hurt him badly. The villagers' suspicions had wounded him too.

He thought about Meg. She had let them out of the cottage. Then he'd heard the click and shot of bolts being thrown and the cottage being locked up tight. He hadn't asked her what she was frightened of. Perhaps it was simply the transition from London to living in the middle of nowhere that generated fear. He knew people who couldn't stand the silence and emptiness of the land. For him, it was the opposite. He couldn't last more than a day in the city without feeling claustrophobic.

He sat in the darkness, not shutting the curtains, letting his table lamp provide a circle of pooled yellow light. She wasn't married. Now why did that make him feel just a little happier?

# 5

Meg put her pen down with satisfaction. She stretched her arms above her head to loosen the knotted muscles in her shoulders. She had been hunched over her desk writing all morning, but it was worth it. She was pleased with her article. She'd been commissioned to write a piece on how to move house from city to country with a personal angle. Now her mind was full of other ideas she could submit to magazines, based on her recent personal experiences of Devon. She smiled. It helped having the wonderful view from her window. She worked from the living room and had set up her desk to look out on the quiet lane. There were no distractions then from her work. No one walked past, and only birds provided movement and song as they flitted amongst the hedgerow shrubs. It was as good as if she faced a blank wall. If there was a safety, too, in knowing she'd see anyone approach the cottage, then this was unvoiced, perhaps even subconscious. It was a week since she'd seen the intruder in the barn, who'd turned out to be an innocent boy, and as the days went by her fears had subsided.

Katie was once again staying over at another of Jane's sleepovers. Meg had the uncomfortable feeling that Tabby had suggested it to her daughter to help out. Meg had told Tabby how difficult it was to get any work done when Katie was around. She wanted her mother to play and chat with her, quite naturally, but Meg needed to work if she was to have any money coming in. What she really ought to do was get Katie a nursery place in the village, but she was reluctant to do so. Maybe after the schools' summer break was over she'd look into it. But until then she'd try to balance entertaining Katie with working from home. With a grimace, Meg admitted to herself that so far she hadn't got the balance right.

'Don't be silly, darling.' Tabby had waved her concerns away with flapping hands. 'Jane loves having Katie to stay. To be honest you're doing me a favour. Have you any idea how long the holidays feel when you've four kids underfoot every single day?'

Well no, she hadn't. She had only a singleton. Meg would've loved to have the same friendly chaos that reigned in the Shaw household. The kitchen where she sat sipping coffee with Tabby was strewn with items of cast-aside clothing, two footballs, a half-completed jigsaw and a large inflatable fish. Ellen and her best friend were crouched on the floor with tiny bottles of nail varnish, painting each other's nails. Jane and Katie were outside, planting a garden with tiny trowels and a packet of sunflower seeds that Tabby had given them. The boys, Jacob and William, had disappeared with a gang of local boys to play a football game over on the common, but not before eight of them had been fed and watered with orange juice and slices of lemon cake hot from Tabby's oven.

It was all so ordinary and homely and comforting, but Meg didn't have anything like it. She was trying her best to provide a loving stable home for Katie, but was she succeeding? She didn't know. Katie seemed happy. She never asked about her father. But could a mother who had five locks on her front door be considered ordinary? Was she going to make Katie into a nervous child by not letting her run free on her own in the fields outside the cottage? Sometimes Meg's own thoughts drove her crazy and then she flew to Tabby.

'Am I imposing on you horribly?' she asked honestly. 'I mean, friendship's meant to be give and take, but all I seem to be doing is taking and taking.'

'That's nonsense,' Tabby said briskly, pushing another slice of cake across the table to her. 'Here, eat that. It'll do you good.'

Meg laughed. 'See what I mean? You're mothering me and I'm letting you.'

Tabby grinned. 'Maybe I am. But you need it. You're still too thin and I can tell you're still looking over your shoulder for Phillip. I'm right, aren't I?'

'Less now than when I arrived,' Meg said. 'I'm beginning to think you were right and that I imagined it. After all, why would he watch me and phone me? As you said, he's got his new wife Leila now. No, I was being daft. I feel much more relaxed this week.'

'It's the country air. Makes one sleepy and quite cosy. So no more apologies for leaving Katie with us, do you hear? We love having her and Jane would be cross if she didn't get to have her little sleepovers with her new best friend.'

'I wish I'd been stronger and insisted on seeing my friends. I shouldn't have let Phillip dictate to me so much. I should've fought harder to keep in touch with you in those days.'

'If I'd known what your life was like back then, wild horses wouldn't have kept me from barging in to see you.'

'Thank you Tabby, for all you've done.' Meg tried not to sound tearful.

'Here, here, it's over. The past is finished with. You and Katie have a wonderful future ahead of you here in Burley. Not quite the centre of the universe, but a good little place nonetheless,' Tabby said cheerfully.

Meg nodded. Tabby was right. She had to forget Phillip and that awful period of her life. For Katie's sake she had to look straight ahead into tomorrow and make it good. Buoyed up by that conviction she left the Shaws' home happily, planning to make the next day full with her work, the ideas for her article bubbling up in her head already.

Now, with a morning's work behind her, Meg felt she deserved a break. Then she'd put in a few more hours until Tabby dropped Katie off. It was another lovely dry sunny day so without bothering with a jacket, she simply walked out of the back gate and into the field. She had no particular destination in mind. It didn't matter. It was good to get some fresh air before she had to sit at her desk again.

If she was home in London then her break would've taken her down onto the Tottenham Court Road, where she'd have wandered in and out of all the little shops finding curiosities and coming back with a bunch of fresh coriander, a bag of rice half-priced, and spiced chicken on impulse for dinner. She still missed the city. It wasn't as easy here to get to the shops for what she wanted. The village store didn't run to exotic foods and the big supermarket was a good twenty minutes' drive into the next town.

Her feet took her slowly up the field on the soft, sheep-mown grass and over a rough wooden stile onto moorland. Here there was springy purple and green heather and occasional tufts of white cotton. The heather was scratchy on her ankles and her feet slipped in unsuitable sandals, but she kept going up until she reached the low crest of the hill. From there she saw the sea and glimpsed the village houses. She was about to turn back when she found a faint path through the heather. Following it, she went diagonally back down the gradient and across another stile into a wide field. This one was clearly not in use by the farm because the grass was long, and here and there little trees sprouted from the ground.

She wandered along until the path faded away and then stopped. Perhaps that was a sign she ought to go back. She had plenty to get through before Katie got home. She looked up, ready for a last view before returning, and straight into the surprised gaze of Garth Winter. He was coming through a gate on the opposite side of the field. Meg registered that he actually looked pleased to see her. He was carrying a canvas rucksack and a pair of binoculars. He hesitated, then gave her a brief wave. She raised her hand in return, then walked to meet him.

'Hello, Meg. Lovely day.'

Meg. Not Mrs Lyons. His visit to her last week with Ben had changed something between them for the better. She'd been only too glad to help tend Ben's cut leg. Had Garth also needed reassurance that he was doing the right thing taking the boy in? No, she was reading too much into that. She was his nearest neighbour, that was all.

'Mr Winter.' She inclined her head in greeting. No, that wasn't fair. 'Garth,' she corrected with a smile. 'I hope I'm not trespassing.'

He lifted the rucksack. 'Not at all. This field is fallow. Please walk here any time you wish.'

There was a silence then. The awkwardness she felt with him hadn't completely gone. He wasn't a man that welcomed chat, she felt. In turn, that clammed her up. With Tabby she could talk for hours, but now her words dried up.

'I should really get back,' she said

self-consciously. 'I'm meant to be working. This is a small break in my day.'

He sat down on the grass and opened up the rucksack. It was filled with little tinfoil packages and a flask. He looked up at her. 'Have you had lunch?' He unwrapped some of the parcels to reveal wedges of cheese, oatcakes and a tub of cherry tomatoes. 'Would you like to join me?'

Meg's stomach rumbled treacherously. She'd forgotten about eating. Now, seeing the food he was laying out on a tea towel, she could definitely eat. 'Are you sure? I don't want to eat up your picnic and leave you hungry.'

'I always pack far too much just for me. If you don't wish to, I won't be offended. If you're working.'

Meg sat down. 'No, I'd like to, thanks.' The old stiffness in his voice had shadowed his last comments. She didn't want to lose the small rapport they'd developed. Besides, the thought of a summer picnic, however small, was appealing.

'Is this a favourite spot of yours?' she asked as he unpacked the flask and set it upright on a convenient flat stone.

'Yes.' He stopped as if he'd say no more. Then, after a moment, he went on. 'My wife and I liked to picnic here. This is Anna's Field. Named for her.'

'I'm sorry,' Meg said quietly.

Garth didn't look at her. His gaze focused out to the sea and the horizon. His voice was bitterly hard when he spoke. 'You heard then. I suppose I shouldn't be surprised. Village gossip is fast and efficient. It's judge and jury too. You'll have the full story, I've no doubt, with all the lurid colouring in.'

'Tabby told me your wife died in a car accident. That's all. I don't know anyone else in the village and I don't like listening to idle gossip.'

Garth sighed. His head dropped to his chest. Then he raised it and looked at her. There was such pain in his dark blue eyes that she almost gasped.

'Now I'm the one who's sorry,' he said quietly. 'Yes, Anna died in a car accident. It was four years ago and I should be at peace with it by now, or so I believe.'

'What happened?' Meg asked, then wished she hadn't when his face darkened. She thought he wouldn't speak. He flung the remains of an oatcake into the grass almost angrily.

'It was a winter's night and the weather was foul. Anna and I . . . we'd been at a party. Friends in the village.' He paused. 'The rain was coming down in sheets and there was sleet and hail too. I should've waited until it passed, but there had been an incident at the party . . . well, anyway, Anna was insistent she wanted to get home. So we drove into the storm.' He shook his head, immersed in his memories. 'I didn't see the dog until it was too late. The next thing I remember is waking up in the hospital. Anna was dead, while I had escaped with cuts and bruises.'

Meg shivered despite the heat of the sun. It was a horrible story. Poor, poor

Garth. And poor, unfortunate Anna.

Garth shook his head and attempted a smile. 'Come, I shouldn't be spoiling the day with my problems. Let's talk about something else. I wanted to thank you for helping me with Ben's leg last week.'

'I was happy to,' Meg answered, relieved at the change in conversation. Garth's pain was so raw and powerful it had swallowed her up too. Let them move onto something lighter. 'How is Ben? Is he still at the farm?'

'He's helping my manager, Alex, with a few tasks daily. Then he comes back and eats like a horse at my expense.' Garth smiled.

'Has he told you where he came from? And if he's going to go home?'

'Not so far, and I'm not pushing him. If he's eighteen, then it's his business.'

'And if he isn't?' Meg could quite see how Garth, living his own life of solitude, not dependent on others, might allow Ben the same privilege. But she doubted he was as old as he said he was. If he was younger, then someone somewhere would be out of their mind with worry about him.

Garth lifted his shoulders. 'I can't force the truth from him. Whatever he's run from, it'll mend in time; then we'll see.'

There was sense in that, Meg agreed. She wondered if Garth's conviction that Ben's problems would mend with time extended to his own life. Four years of shutting people out was a long haul for anyone. Yet seeing the anguish in his expression, Meg didn't think his own pain had healed with all those days gone.

A brown bird flew up from behind a clump of rushes at the bottom of the field. It sang in rich warbling tones as it ascended. 'Woodlark,' Garth said, handing her the binoculars.

She tried to see through them but it was blurred and there was no sign of the bird. Garth took them back and adjusted the eyepiece. Then she lifted them again. It was difficult to match where the bird was hovering with where the binoculars should aim. Suddenly Garth's warm hands were over hers, moving the lenses to the right place. Meg couldn't concentrate on the bird anymore. She was too aware of the roughness of his palms and the male strength of him behind her. In confusion she let them drop. Garth caught them easily.

'I've never used binoculars before,' she said stupidly. She moved away from him, hoping it wasn't too obvious the effect he had on her. Why was her body behaving this way? She couldn't be attracted to him. She'd no intention of being attracted to any man. She and Katie had a life together and that was the way she intended it to stay. She might admit to *liking* Garth Winter now, but that was as far as it went.

'That's a terrible confession. Comes from living in the city!'

Meg looked up at him quickly. He gave her a grin. He was teasing her. Garth Winter was teasing her!

'Well as I'm going back there tomorrow, who knows what other horrible habits I'll pick up while I'm there,' she joked.

He quirked an eyebrow. 'Going back? For long?' Was there a hint of disappointment in his question? Was he going to miss her?

'Just for the day,' she replied. 'I need to move the rest of my belongings out of my flat. Not many things, thank goodness, but my new tenant moves in this week so I want it nice for her.'

Meg's aunt's estate was a large enough inheritance to allow her to keep the Tottenham flat. In the back of her thoughts was the comfort of knowing that if it didn't work out living in Primrose Cottage in the back of beyond, she could always go back to London.

'You'll enjoy going back.'

'Yes and no,' she said. She began to repack the rucksack with the remains of the picnic, avoiding his questioning look.

'Why did you come to live in such a tiny village as Burley?' There was a pause, then Garth shook his head.

'Sorry, I don't know why I'm being so nosy. Forget I asked. None of my business.' His voice was clipped, the way she remembered from her first meeting with him, the day Katie disappeared. She replied quickly, not wanting to lose the rapport that had been built between them.

'Not at all. It's a good question. I'm . . . I'm escaping from my previous life.' There, that was the bald truth. He didn't say anything so she went on. 'My husband, my exhusband, was a difficult man to live with.'

'Hence the locks on your front door? Are you afraid of him?'

Meg zipped the rucksack and gave it to him. All of a sudden she wanted to confide in Garth. All her fears and worries shared like water rushing down a cataract, but she didn't know him well enough. She'd revised her original impression of him. He might like to keep his own company, but he wasn't the cantankerous hermit she'd painted him to be. It wasn't fair of her to burden someone else with her problems. Besides, even her best friend Tabby had told her she was imagining a lot of it. If it was all in her head then she had to sort it out herself.

'City girls are used to locks on their doors,' she told him lightly. 'Thanks for the lovely picnic but I must get back now. Katie will be home very soon.'

They walked back together across Anna's Field until their ways parted and the split track led either up to Winter Farm or over the stile and down the grassy gradient to the back of Primrose Cottage. Garth gave a little nod, hitched the rucksack more firmly onto his shoulder and went on to the big house. Meg watched him, then turned down the slope. They'd shared more than a picnic today. Somehow they had reached an understanding of each other. She felt his absence as she went in through the back door.

# 6

'Lots of sand, Mummy, look.' Katie clapped her hands together in delight and pressed her button nose up against the car window.

'Yes Katie kid, you're right, there is. That's Burley beach. We'll go and explore it together this week, I promise,' Meg laughed, happy at Katie's obvious pleasure.

'Where are we going?' Katie asked, turning in her car seat to look at her mother.

'We're going to London today, back to the flat. You can help me tidy it up for the new lady who's going to live there.'

'Are we coming back to Booley?' Katie asked anxiously.

'Burley,' Meg corrected automatically. 'Do you want to come back?'

'Yes, yes, Jane is here.'

Meg blew a silent breath of relief. Katie was settling in well. She seemed very happy at the cottage and with her frequent visits to see Jane. It made the move much easier on Meg, knowing that Katie was content.

'Is Kanga there?' Katie said.

Kanga, a moth-eaten ginger cat, belonged to Meg's Tottenham neighbour. She'd forgotten how attached Katie had been to it.

'We'll see when we get there. That'll be nice, won't it,' Meg said with forced cheerfulness.

She was not looking forward to going back to her flat. It was a reminder of an unhappy period in her life. If it wasn't for the new tenant, she'd never have returned. How strange the difference a few weeks could make in a life. The time living in Burley seemed so much longer; it was such a different environment. She hadn't realised just what a change it was for the better.

Yet as they approached London and the roads became wider and busier, and the fields and woods vanished beneath concrete and bricks, Meg brightened. She loved the hustle and bustle of it all. There was so much to see. There were people and vehicles everywhere, everyone busy about their lives, the whole scene shot with a kaleidoscope of colours. She'd forgotten how much she loved this old city. Meg pulled a face at herself in the driver's mirror. She had a split personality, that was for sure: one minute pining for Primrose Cottage and dreading the flat in Tottenham, the next urging her car on with anticipation into the urban arteries, Burley village quite forgotten.

The M25 was surprisingly light on traffic and the Ford Fiesta whizzed along it, and then they were on the road into Tottenham. Now Meg slowed the car, crawling along the narrow London streets behind a large white van with a roof rack full of rolled carpets. With relief she peeled off onto the side street that took them round the edge of a large public park and on to the flat.

There was one small space left for parking on the road and she managed to reverse her car into it. She released Katie's seatbelt and lifted her out onto the pavement.

'I'm hungry. Can I get crisps?' Katie whined.

'Maybe,' Meg said distractedly.

Her thoughts were taken up by the sight of the flat in front of them. It was the top half of a house in a terraced row. The house was made of traditional London red brick, much of which was pitted with age and neglect. The paint was peeling from the white windowsills and the tiny front yard was full of litter. Meg's spirits sank. Somehow she'd forgotten just how awful the reality was. There was a loud pulse of music coming from an open window further up the terrace, and shouting from another where a heated argument was clearly going on.

'Kanga!' Katie ran across the road to where a scrawny ginger tom had leapt onto the low brick wall. She began to stroke it and talk to it in a kind, soft voice. The cat rubbed against her, tail straight up in welcome.

The nearest front door opened and Meg's old neighbour leaned out. ''allo, love. Are you coming back to live 'ere then? Good thing if you did. See, them youths've thrown their rubbish where they like. Shameful, it is. Shameful.'

'Hello, no I'm just here for the day. I've got a lady moving in at the end of this week so I'm here to tidy up. I'll get rid of the litter.'

'Bless you. I'd do it meself, but me back's giving me awful gyp, and me son's never here. Found himself a new girlfriend, he 'as, and moved out.'

'Oh dear, I'm sorry to hear that.' Meg got her keys out and moved towards her own front door. Her neighbour was a lovely woman but inclined to long, deliberating conversations. But her next comment made Meg freeze.

'I forgot, there was a man 'ere asking for you. Lovely looking chap 'e was, too. An admirer, is he?'

'What did you tell him?'

'Well 'e was ever so nice, very chatty like. Asked all about you and the little one. Said he was a friend who'd lost touch wiv you. I gave him your new address. Did 'e get hold of you then?'

Meg pulled Katie away from the cat and fumbled with her front door key. She glanced around.

'Did I do wrong? Everything all right, love?'

'Yes, it's fine. Thanks for keeping an eye on the place. We must get on now with tidying.' Meg's face felt tight with the façade of calmness. It wasn't her neighbour's fault. The 'friend' could only be Phillip. So she had seen him that day on the High Street. But why was he keeping tabs on her? Why wasn't he content with his new life and Leila Graham? Her thoughts rattled like a storm on metal. She pulled Katie fast up the stairs and jabbed the key into the battered lock. Once inside the flat, she slammed the door shut and bolted it.

'Mummy, you're hurting me,' Katie wailed. She rubbed her wrist where Meg had held it tightly.

'Sorry, darling.' Meg knelt, contrite, and hugged her daughter. 'Mummy's a bit tired and silly, that's all. Why don't you go and look in our bedroom, see if you've left any old toys?'

The place smelt empty, with an absence of cooking smells and laundry freshness, spray polish and everyday use. Instead, even after only two weeks, there was a faint odour of dust in the hot, stuffy air. Meg opened the window and a blast of even hotter air laced with diesel, melting tarmac and rap music floated in. She shook her head in dismay but left it open anyway. There wasn't much to do, she saw with a sense of relief. She went into the rooms, which were fairly bare except for the carpet or lino floors. Here and there were small items that had been missed in the move. She gathered them in a pile at the door.

'No toys,' Katie said sadly.

'That's good news. It means they're all safe at home.' Meg smiled and kissed her.

'Is this home too?'

'Not anymore. We're happy at Primrose Cottage, aren't we?'

Katie stared at her doubtfully. Now she was back in the flat, her feelings were different. She'd spent most of her short life living here. This was what was familiar.

'The cottage is a holiday,' Katie said triumphantly as if she'd come up with the solution to a very difficult question. She beamed up at Meg.

'Katie . . . '

The doorbell rang shrilly. Meg jumped, then gave a shaky laugh. It was probably her neighbour with more news she'd forgotten to share. Without thinking, she flicked back the bolt and opened it.

A tall, dark-haired man stood there. Before Meg had time to react, Phillip had walked into the hall and shut the door firmly behind him. She took a step back, instinctively shielding Katie.

'Hello, Meg. Welcome back.'

'What are you doing here?' she whispered. Her throat was dry and her chest tight. Phillip was as film-star handsome as ever. His hair was thick and wavy and she noticed it was winged with grey, which made him look even more distinguished. He was wearing an expensive well-cut suit and a blue silk tie. She wondered if he'd come to them from his office.

'That's not much of a greeting to an old friend.' He laid an emphasis on the word 'friend' and Meg was reminded that he'd duped her trusting neighbour to extract information on her.

'What do you want?' she asked more forcefully.

'I wanted to see you and find out how you've been since you deserted me.' Phillip spoke mildly but there was a glitter in his brown eyes that made the little hairs on the back of her neck rise up.

'I didn't desert you,' Meg said. 'We both know the marriage wasn't working. You drove me away with your drinking.' *And your unreasonable, dominating behaviour.* But she didn't say it.

He shrugged casually. 'Water under the bridge. I forgive you.'

'Who's that man, Mummy?' Katie peeked out from behind Meg's leg.

Phillip crouched down and gave her his most charming smile. Katie returned it prettily.

'Tell her who it is, Meg,' he said.

'This is your daddy,' she said, the words like sawdust in her mouth.

It wasn't how she'd wanted to explain to Katie about her lack of a daddy. When she was older and able to understand, Meg had envisaged sitting down with her and telling her gently. Although she knew she'd never tell Katie that Phillip hadn't wanted her.

Katie stared at Phillip with round eyes but didn't take a step away from Meg. He beckoned her forward but she didn't budge. Abruptly he stood, his attention no longer on the small child. Instead he cast his gaze round the flat.

'Why on earth would you choose to

live here when we had our beautiful house at Kew?'

'How did you find me?' Meg asked, ignoring his question.

'It was relatively easy. I had a private detective locate you. You left quite a paper trail, I'm afraid.'

'So you've known all along where we were living. It was you I saw that day on the High Street. I don't understand. You've remarried, you don't need me or love me anymore, so why?'

'You're right, I don't love you. In fact I don't think I ever did,' Phillip said matter-of-factly. 'You are a very beautiful woman, Meg, and we made a perfect pair. But you spoiled it by running off. It didn't look good to my investors or my business partners, and didn't help my position in society, to be quite honest. Thank goodness Leila has shown more lady-like restraint. Quite mended that humiliating period of my life. But you don't simply leave me. I didn't give you permission to go. I know everything about you, Meg. And I always will.'

Her skin prickled icily despite the heat of the room. Phillip spoke in a calm, measured tone but his words echoed with madness. Holding Katie's hand, she edged round him and opened the front door with a shaky hand. Then with more courage than she felt, she gestured out to the stone stairway.

'Please leave now.'

Surprisingly, Phillip made no protest. He smiled and dipped his head as though in polite acknowledgement. His polished, hand-made leather shoes made no sound as he strode past her and out of the flat. Meg held her breath. She was ready to shut the door and bolt it when he put up a hand, palm flat against it. She couldn't shut it without an unseemly tussle. As her heart thumped painfully and she thought of her mobile phone inside the pocket of her handbag and out of reach on the living room table, Phillip spoke mockingly.

'Primrose Cottage in the tiny Devon village of Burley. A wonderful choice, Meg, for your escape from London.

Very peaceful, very safe. I might pop in and visit you some day. After all, Katie has a right to know her father.'

He turned smartly on his heel before she could react and was gone. Meg's legs gave out beneath her and she fell to the hall floor on her knees. Katie knelt too, copying her. Meg shivered with a flu-like intensity. She gathered Katie in to her and hugged her until her muscles calmed and the spasms passed.

'Are you sick?' Katie asked. She felt Meg's forehead with a sticky hand. Meg managed a reassuring smile. She mustn't let Phillip get under her skin. She had to act normally for Katie's sake. She'd mull it all over later when they got home.

'No, I'm okay now, darling. Let's get busy with our sorting. I'm going to get the bin bags.'

She cleared the rubbish out of the garden with Katie's help. Kanga sat and watched them from the wall. The neighbour came out with a cup of tea for Meg and a carton of juice for Katie and chatted while she filled the bags with old take-away polystyrene, plastic bottles and crisp packets. All the while, like the repeating chug of a train on a track, she thought, *Phillip knows where we live, Phillip knows where we live.* The taste of bile caught in her throat and she coughed. No amount of tea could remove the bitterness. Her dream of a new life crumbled like the red grit eroding from the terraced houses' brick. Were they never to be free of him?

*   *   *

They got back to the cottage late in the evening. Meg lifted a limp and quietly snoring Katie from the car.

'Let me help.'

Katie's weight was taken from her and she looked up into Garth's crinkled blue eyes. 'I was passing by,' he explained.

Meg glanced at the lane and the gate and back at him.

'Okay, I was checking to make sure you were back safely,' Garth admitted sheepishly.

'I'm glad you did,' Meg said feelingly.

Garth laid the sleeping child gently on the sofa and turned to her. 'What happened?' He moved towards her then stopped. Meg almost cried out for him to continue, to put his arms around her, to feel his strength surround her. She needed comfort in that moment desperately. Never had she felt so alone. Instead she sank down onto the sofa beside Katie. Garth sat on the near armchair and waited.

She swallowed nervously. Phillip's unexpected visit was vivid, his words playing over and over in her mind. 'My ex-husband found us.'

'Found you? He wasn't meant to know where you were?'

Meg found herself telling him everything that she'd told Tabby about her sham of a marriage and her fear of Phillip and that final fleeing to Tottenham. When she'd finished her sorry tale she rubbed her face tiredly. 'The thing is, he said something odd just before he left,' she said, remembering.

'Which was?' Garth prompted. Somehow his hand was covering hers and she felt the warmth and strength of his grasp. It felt good.

'That Katie has a right to get to know her father.'

'And you don't agree?' Garth asked. She couldn't tell from his voice what his opinion was. Besides, he didn't know Phillip. She laughed bitterly. 'I happen to agree whole-heartedly with the sentiment. However, I spent the first year of Katie's life trying to interest Phillip in his own daughter without success. In the two years apart, he's never tried to get access to her, which he could have done through the lawyer. So why now?'

'Perhaps he's finally realised what an important relationship it is.'

Meg wondered if Garth was thinking of his own lost possibilities with Anna. Tabby hadn't mentioned children at Winter Farm and neither had Garth. Had he wanted to be a father? She didn't know him well enough to ask him.

'He knows where we live,' she

repeated bleakly.

Primrose Cottage was no longer the safe haven she'd created. It never had been. The phone call that first night had been Phillip, she was certain. It was the same as those she'd got sporadically in the Tottenham flat. The empty envelope was his way of mocking her sense of security.

'He has no power over you, Meg,' Garth said. 'Only what you grant him.'

She rose from her seat agitatedly. 'You don't know him. You don't know what he's capable of. What if he arrives here? What if he wants custody of Katie?' She was shaking with emotion. Garth rose too and moved swiftly to her, catching her fluttering hands in his and stilling them. She stared into his blue gaze, like midnight velvet, darkening even as she watched. Afterwards she wasn't sure who moved first but then his lips covered hers, warm and mobile. Their kiss was at first tentative, then quickly molten. Meg's heartbeat quickened and she moved into the mould of his body instinctively. Just as she lost herself in the wonder of the taste and touch of him, it was gone.

Garth was breathing heavily. He touched a finger briefly to her flushed cheek as if with regret. 'I'm sorry. I shouldn't have . . . I'll leave.'

She stood wordlessly while he went, her lips still bruised from his passionate kiss. She touched them with the tip of her tongue, marvelling at what had occurred. She ran to the kitchen and saw his tall figure striding up the slope to the red tiled roof, barely visible in the fading light. He didn't look back.

When she'd tucked Katie into bed with Belly Bear and put out the bedroom light, gone downstairs and locked the mortise and finally sat alone in the living room with a glass of ruby red wine, she decided it was for the best. They had been taken over by the charged nature of the moment. He felt sorry for her. She was desperate for comfort. That was all.

Her dreams were full of danger. A

dark shape was following her and she knew if it caught her up she was doomed. Just beyond the horizon there was hope and salvation if only she could reach it. A shrill bird was crying over and over, an omen of bad luck. She sat bolt upright in bed. Her alarm clock shone its digital hours. It was the middle of the night. Downstairs the telephone continued to ring.

# 7

The lake was a smooth, glassy aqua-marine and the sky swirled magically with the pinks of early sunset. Garth's paintbrush swept over the canvas, thick with coloured oil, hand and imagination moving as one to create a perfect land-scape. He was absorbed in his work, the outside world reduced to a mere back-ground hum. There was a sense of complete satisfaction in what he was doing and he knew this was going to be one of his best creations ever.

There was a series of loud thumps behind him. His concentration shattered and Garth put down the brush reluc-tantly. Ben rubbed his head sleepily. His T-shirt and jeans were wrinkled and his large, bony feet were bare. 'I'm not doing it,' he announced flatly.

Garth didn't reply. He turned back to the canvas. The paint glistened on it.

Oil pooled under the brush where it lay on the palette. There was the slap of Ben's feet on the tiles, then the gush of tap water and the sharp click of the kettle turned on at the switch. Garth sighed and gave up. He rose and went into the kitchen, leaning on the wall to watch the boy spread a slice of bread with a mountain of orange marmalade. Garth had taken Meg's advice and tried to persuade Ben to contact his family.

*Meg.* Even the sound of her name gave him a warm glow. Was it possible to feel this good about a woman he'd only known a fortnight? He thought of their passionate embrace. It had come out of nowhere and turned into something brief but very special. It had ignited a heat within him for her. After four years of self-imposed exile from other people, he was ready to let someone inside his armour. It felt dangerous and reckless but oh so *right*. He felt alive.

'You can't make me phone my parents,' Ben said in a surly tone. 'I'm an adult. I don't have to do what you say or what anyone else does either.'

Garth raised his palms in mock surrender. 'Hold your fire, I'm coming out.' He reached for a slice of bread and slid it into the toaster. 'Ben, nobody's going to make you do anything you don't want to, okay? You can stay here as long as you want. All I want you to promise me is that you'll think about contacting your folks. Is that fair?'

The truth was that Garth had asked Alex Cranborn to make discreet enquiries in Burley and beyond as to whether there was a missing teenager alert. Alex had come back to Garth shaking his head. 'No, Mr Winter, there don't be nobody round here missing a boy. Reckon he came down from the cities. If he's a bother to you I can take him to the authorities.'

'Thanks, Alex, but there's plenty of space here. I don't mind him staying until he decides what to do.'

In fact, Garth had got quite used to the sounds of another human being at Winter Farm. Ben wasn't much of a talker, and liked his own company. But it was pleasant to have a companion at meals and at the end of the day, to walk round the property. He hadn't missed people since Anna died and hadn't wanted them, if he was honest; but now, well . . . if Ben went he'd notice the gap.

Alex raised a grizzled eyebrow at his answer but didn't ask further. He tipped his flat cap at Garth politely and left.

'I'll think about it,' Ben agreed through a mouthful of food.

Garth pushed the plate of toast across to him and they ate together, standing at the sink and looking out at the day.

'I'm going to get a dog,' Ben announced when the plate was empty.

'Can I ask why?'

'Alex was telling me how useful they are. Man's best friend and all that, yeah, but on a farm the dogs earn their keep. If I'm going to be a farmer someday, I should get one.'

Garth took the plate and rinsed it

under the hot water tap. 'It's a big responsibility,' he said.

'I can look after it. Alex'll show me. I'm learning lots from him about farm management.'

Garth looked at the boy. Ben's face was eager. Garth remembered his own younger years when everything had the keen edge of possibility and the world was a positive and magical place. He smiled at Ben. 'I believe Alex knows just where to get your puppy. Perhaps if you get one, he'll stop trying to persuade me that I need one.'

Ben whooped in delight and punched the air. Garth grinned at his obvious happiness. It lit up the morning. Ben clattered up the stairs and he heard the patter of the shower and loud, tuneless singing. The house needed noise, he realised. For far too long it had been encased in a wrap of silence, self-imposed. If only he and Anna had had children. That thought still stung. How foolishly confident he'd been with his plan of having four lively children, amongst them a son who'd take over Winter Farm in due course. It had all withered with Anna's death. No — if he were truthful, his plans had rotted and died well before that. Anna's problems were too all-encompassing for anything else to survive.

\* \* \*

'Would you mind if we invited Meg and her daughter to come with us?' Garth asked Ben.

Alex Cranborn had been telephoned and it was arranged that Ben and Garth would go up that morning to view the puppies at a farm on the moors. When that was settled, Garth thought again of Meg's fears. How well-founded were they? How likely was it that her ex-husband was really stalking her? *You don't know him. You don't know what he's capable of*, she'd said. While that was true, Garth doubted that Phillip would really carry out any threats he'd made. Wasn't he simply taunting her?

He sounded like a nasty piece of work. It wouldn't do any harm for Garth to keep watch over her until her fears faded. If that gave him an excuse to be near her, then that was okay too.

Ben nodded. 'Yeah, I like Meg. It'd be cool if she joined us to see the dogs.'

When Meg opened the door to them, she had bruised patches under her eyes and Garth guessed she hadn't slept well. He fought an urge to pull her to him and hold her tightly, to kiss away the shadows. 'We were hoping you might join us on a day trip,' he said instead.

Meg started to shake her head but Katie pushed by her legs and beamed up at him. 'Yes please. I'd like a day trip.'

'Where are you headed?' Meg asked, taking Katie's hand.

'I'm getting a dog,' Ben told her.

Katie squealed and jumped up and down. 'A dog, a dog! I want to see the doggy, Mummy. Please.'

Meg laughed and the strain left her face. Garth felt the warmth of her laughter touch him. Katie was asking

Ben to describe the dog and he in turn had hunkered down to speak to her. It was going to be all right.

The farm which had the litter of puppies was a good drive away up in the moors. Garth insisted on driving them, despite Meg saying she and Katie would follow them in her car. He wondered if she always had to be so independent. In any case, she looked so exhausted, it mightn't be safe for her to drive. He didn't mention that, but suggested it'd be more relaxed if they all travelled together.

He almost missed the turnoff. They drove along a single-track road laid like an undulating grey ribbon onto the moorland. There were occasional tracks leading off from it, but faintly, as though they could at any moment disappear back into the soil. A herd of sturdy ponies pulled at the stunted grass and trotted away when the car went past.

'What a wild land,' Meg commented, looking out at the ponies. 'Is that the place?'

Garth followed the direction of her pointing finger and saw a group of grey buildings low in a hollow of the land. He stopped the car and reversed it back a few yards.

'Well spotted, and here's the track.' He grinned over at her and she smiled back.

Did she know how gorgeous she was? Her dark hair was shiny as it spilled down onto her shoulders, and her grey eyes were large and fringed with black lashes. Even pale with fatigue, she was beautiful. Was she remembering their kiss? Did she regret it? Looking back at her now, he most certainly did not. He glanced at her lips. They were softly pink and full and eminently kissable. He could lean over and touch them with his own. A physical tug of desire leaned him towards her. Meg looked away and Garth stopped. Laughter in the back of the car, where Ben was showing Katie how to cat's-cradle with a piece of string, brought him back to reality.

'This is it,' he said heartily, 'I'll park up here. Are you ready?'

In the end, they left the car in front of the farm house beside two other cars, both slightly battered. Near them were old metal barriers and the hulks of sheds full of machinery and hay. The house itself was a dark, gloomy grey with small windows and a smear of mud along the side of the wall. They got out of the car and were hit by the smell of manure. Meg wrinkled her nose and spoke in a low voice.

'It's quite different from Winter Farm.'

'This is a dairy farm,' Garth said. 'More pungent.' They shared a smile.

'Where's Ben's puppy?' Katie piped up, tugging at Meg's blouse.

'I don't know, Katie kid. Let's go and find it, shall we?' Meg kissed her.

'I'm going with Ben,' Katie announced. 'I'm going to help him choose.' She ran over to him, her red wellies slapping in the mud.

'Sorry, Ben. Do you mind?' Meg asked.

'Not at all. I'll need Katie's expert opinion,' Ben said nicely.

The tall youth and the little girl led the way to where a man had appeared from the edge of the buildings. Garth walked with Meg in companionable silence. It felt good being with her. He'd chosen to shut himself away from other people for so long, denying the loneliness that followed, telling himself he was happy to be on his own. He'd had time to mourn for Anna in those four years. But now, with the chatter from Ben and Katie and the friendship of the woman by his side, he realised how deeply alone he'd been. He couldn't go back to that. Not now.

'You've come about the collies,' the farmer said. 'Alex said you'd be over.' He jerked his head towards the nearest shed. They followed his bulky form into the cool darkness to where a black and white dog lay sprawling on the dirt with five puppies tumbling around her.

*   *   *

'Fluffy.'

'That's a rabbit's name.'

'Spot.'

'He hasn't got a spot. Sorry, Katie, try again.'

Garth and Meg sat on a bench in a picnic spot on the moors while Ben, Katie and the unnamed puppy lay on the grass together. They'd all been glad to get the puppy and leave the dour farmer and the smell of the farm behind. Garth had stopped at a village shop and bought them cartons of drinks and snacks before they found the bench under a cluster of trees.

'Do you think Ben misses his family?' Meg said quietly. They were far enough away to converse without Ben hearing them.

'I hope he thinks about them. Maybe being with Katie will make him want to contact them.'

'Whatever made him leave, I wonder,' Meg said.

Then Ben and Katie joined them again, Ben holding the wriggling animal. He put it down and it tumbled in excitement before galloping off with Katie after it.

'Katie's going to help me train her,' Ben grinned. 'Teach her some puppy manners.'

'Thanks for being so good with her,' Meg said. 'Don't let her boss you though. She can be a little madam.' This was said so fondly that Meg's love for her daughter shone through. Garth felt encircled by it, sitting with her.

'I have a little sister, a bit older than Katie,' Ben said.

'Oh Ben, why don't you get in touch with your family. They must be so worried about you,' Meg cried.

Ben shook his head. 'They don't want me.' He stood up, indicating the conversation was over. His expression was closed and mutinous. Meg opened her mouth as if she'd say more, but Garth closed his hand over hers and squeezed it gently. She nodded to him, but there was distress in her grey eyes that he wanted to kiss away. Her sweet nature drew him to her even more closely. She was tender and loving to all around her, he realised. What a fool Phillip was! How could he have let Meg go? How could he have treated her so badly? If Garth had been Meg's husband he'd have given her the world.

The realisation drenched him like a sudden cascade in spring. There, in that isolated picnic place on the moors with the child's laughter and the dog's high-pitched barking filling the air, he knew that he had fallen in love with Meg. He had never believed in love at first sight. He and Anna had known each other all their lives and had been childhood sweethearts. They'd grown together naturally over the years and it had never been voiced, but simply understood by them and all around them, that one day they'd marry.

But Meg had intrigued him from the moment he set eyes on her, a mere slip of a woman crying in front of the cottage. He'd been too awkward and too contained within his protective shell to approach her, but he was aware of her from then onwards. How could he not love her? She was the most beautiful woman he'd ever met, but that wasn't important compared to her loving and kind personality, and the sheer undeniable and magnetic physical draw she had for him.

Meg frowned and he followed her gaze away from their bench and across the furze and purple-sprigged heather to the road. There was no traffic on the lonely route except for a blue car which had parked next to his. With the sharp sunlight glinting off the windows, it was impossible to see the occupants.

'Why is he just sitting there? Why isn't he getting out?' Meg said.

'Could be someone using their mobile phone,' he suggested. 'If so, they're doing the right thing by stopping. So many accidents are caused by careless drivers talking on their mobiles while driving.'

'It's him. He's following me.' Meg's voice was bleak.

Garth stared at her. 'Are you saying

it's *Phillip*? That he's stalking you?'

Meg looked at him. 'You don't believe me, do you? Tabby thinks I'm imagining it and so do you.'

To be honest, Garth didn't know what to think. Of course he believed Meg's story of how her marriage had been and how she'd fled from her husband. He believed her when she said Phillip had turned up at her flat in Tottenham, but he was inclined to give Phillip the benefit of the doubt for that meeting. Perhaps the man really wanted to get to know his own child and regretted the two years of her life that he'd missed. If Garth had a child, he'd move heaven and earth to be with them. But was Phillip actually following Meg's every move? It didn't matter. Meg's fear of him was real and Garth's protective instinct came to the fore.

'There's one way to find out if it is Phillip,' he said firmly, getting to his feet and beginning to walk towards the blue car.

'Garth!' Meg cried warningly.

The blue car sat there and Garth thought he'd reach it. Whether he was going to peer in the passenger window with a cupped hand or boldly reach for the door handle, he hadn't yet decided. But when he was a few yards away, the car's engine purred into life and the vehicle glided away. He watched it move along the dusty road until it disappeared around the curve.

Meg had reached his side. She was white-faced, but her jaw was tilted up for battle. He felt a tug of admiration for her. She might be afraid of Phillip, but she wasn't going to cower down before him. Garth couldn't help it. He took her to him and kissed her lips. He told himself that it was for comfort and reassurance and friendship. But he was lying to himself. He wanted her. The kiss deepened until she pushed him away. He brushed a knuckle to his mouth and steadied his breath. Meg's cheeks were prettily flushed and a glitter in her gaze reminded him of grey seas lit by diamonds of sunshine on a midsummer's day.

'I'm not sorry for that,' he said, looking straight at her. 'I can't help it. I've fallen in love with you, Meg.'

She gasped.

'Is there any hope for me?' Garth asked.

She half turned from him to stare out across the road and the empty moorland. Then she smiled tremulously.

'I . . . I don't know what to say. I like you very much. But I can't think about this now. I just can't. There's too much uncertainty in my life right now with Phillip . . . I'm so sorry, Garth. I'm sorry.'

# 8

'Who left a pair of trainers in the bath?' Tabby shouted up the stairs. 'If they're not out of there in the next five minutes they're going in the bin.'

There was a whoop and a clatter of heavy feet as the boys dived downstairs. Tabby neatly swerved, picking up three tiny bottles of nail varnish off the floor as she passed and avoiding a stack of books that were masquerading as a fort for an assortment of plastic soldiers.

'Thanks for making the coffee,' Tabby groaned as she sat heavily on the kitchen stool opposite Meg's. 'Pour me a large black one, will you, with extra caffeine. And please tell me that school's going back soon.'

'It's another week until they go back, isn't it?' Meg said. 'I really must organise a nursery place for Katie. I've left it awfully late, but I'm so busy. It feels sort of like autumn now, doesn't it, with the berries on the trees and the fog this morning. The cottage windows keep misting up, but I don't have a moment to clear them, I'm writing so much.'

'How's your work going?' Tabby asked, biting into a ginger biscuit and pushing the plate towards Meg.

'It's like one of those dreams where you're running and running but you never catch up,' Meg said, making a face. 'I'm making just enough cash to get by but I wake up at night worrying about the bills.'

She didn't tell Tabby that she was awake at least one or two hours a night. The phone rang after midnight most nights. Sometimes she ignored it. When she did answer there was nothing but scratchy air to hear. She alternated between saying nothing and shouting down the phone for Phillip to stop tormenting her. Meg felt she was going mad. She was convinced it had been Phillip in the blue car that day but had no proof. Likewise with the phone calls. If Phillip was to blame for them, he'd achieved his aims. She was totally unnerved by the nightly interruptions. He hadn't been in touch otherwise to make good on his comment about getting to know Katie.

'Well, here's something to take your mind off it,' Tabby said cheerfully, and she leant over to fetch a piece of paper which she handed over.

Meg read the flyer. It was for a charity dance and barbecue in the village the following weekend. The contact details were for Tabby.

'Sound like fun?' Tabby said. 'Honestly, Meg, you're looking peaky. You're working too hard, my girl. This dance is just the thing for you.'

'I don't know,' Meg said evasively. 'My weekends are quite busy.'

Tabby snorted rudely. 'What a terrible excuse. No, you're coming along to it and no arguments. It's going to be quite lovely. There'll be waltzes and country dancing, and Maurice is in charge of the barbecue. You have to taste it to believe it. This is an annual event, you see, and the boys have got really good at the whole party food shebang. Besides, I need the moral support of my friends. I'm organising it and I can't have no one turning up.'

'It does sound sort of fun,' Meg agreed, slowly warming to the idea. 'Can I contribute desserts or salads?'

'All that's welcome of course, but you have to contribute something a little more substantial too,' Tabby said with a wicked twinkle to her eye.

'And what might that be?'

Tabby prolonged the tension by insisting Meg pour more coffee and eat another ginger biscuit. Then, through a mouthful of crumbs, she announced cheerfully, 'You have to bring a partner to the dance. Now don't worry, I have the perfect man in mind for you. Ben's work colleague Lawrence is single and apparently very, very nice . . . '

But Meg's mind flashed to Garth. His confession that he was in love with her had sent her reeling. It was completely unexpected. She didn't know how she felt about him. She liked him very much, as she'd told him. But did she love him? It was too soon to tell. She was deeply attracted to him, that she couldn't deny. His kisses melted her insides, leaving her wanting more. Much more. But her emotions were more complicated. Was it right to give way to her physical desires when she had Katie to care for? Her daughter's needs came first and Meg had sworn to give Katie a loving and stable home. It would be too confusing, surely, if Garth became a part of their lives more intimately than just that of a neighbour and friend. Then there was the problem of Phillip. How could she move on with her life and fall in love again when he was there, hovering darkly in the background, not letting her truly go? Also, did she dare to fall in love with another man? Would Garth, too, turn out to be a different person once she gave him her trust? Was there another side to him she hadn't yet seen?

So far, he was kind and helpful and a solid friendship was building up between them, quite besides the almost palpable physical attraction that crackled like electricity along a wire. But she was too cautious to give way to that attraction. She needed to get to know him better; to see whether he was genuine or whether the façade would crack eventually to reveal a different Garth altogether. Before she met Phillip, Meg had never been so wary of people. It was a sadder and wiser woman who'd left that relationship.

'Hello, earth calling Meg.' Tabby snapped her fingertips under Meg's nose, making her jump. 'I asked you whether Lawrence appealed to you at all. Do you mind a bald man?'

'Lawrence?'

Tabby sighed with pretend exasperation. 'You're playing hard to get, is that it? Well you don't need to do that with Lawrence. He's fairly desperate to find a partner.'

Meg laughed. 'Thanks. He sounds like a perfect date for me. So desperate he'll even take Meg Lyons to a village dance.'

'I didn't mean it like that,' Tabby said grumpily, then grinned and brightened when Meg poked her in the ribs. 'You'll do it then? I'll get Ben to phone Lawrence tonight. We can make a foursome.'

'No thanks. I'll bring my own date.'

'Who? Not to be rude, but you don't know anyone else here.'

'I'm going to ask Garth to accompany me.' Meg could think of no one else she'd rather spend an evening with. There had been no awkwardness after she'd told him she couldn't think about him being in love with her. Garth had been very understanding. He'd told her that he could wait. When they joined Ben and Katie it was as if nothing had happened. The rest of the afternoon was fun and relaxed, and on the few occasions she saw him after that, he was his usual pleasant company. There was no pressure from him to be anything other than what she was.

'Garth Winter? You seriously think that Garth would come to the village dance? I'll eat my hat if he does,' Tabby said with raised eyebrows.

'Why shouldn't he come along?' Meg asked defensively. 'He's as much right as anyone else to attend.'

'I'm not saying he hasn't. But he won't leave Winter Farm. If he hasn't left it in four years, why would he start now? Hang on a minute, why would you suggest Garth as a partner? How well do you know him? You're a dark horse, aren't you?' Tabby gave her a hard stare. 'Cough up, chicken.'

'He's my closest neighbour, so of course I've bumped into him a few times,' Meg said. 'We get along okay, so I thought maybe he'd like to get out a bit more.'

'Get along okay,' Tabby echoed with narrowed eyes. 'Hmm, I see. Yes, I think I do see very clearly.'

Meg shifted on her stool. She'd

forgotten how much Tabby liked to be on top of the current gossip. And how good she was at getting it. 'You like him, don't you?' Tabby said triumphantly.

'I like him, but not like that,' Meg protested, wondering if it was true.

There was a crash from the other room and the distraction and procession of guilty children and broken china figurines was a relief to Meg, as it took Tabby's focus away from her. Their chat moved on to other topics as she helped to clear up the mess, and the boys took their football outside to the proper place to play.

It was only when Meg was getting ready to leave that Tabby brought up the subject again. 'He won't come, you know. You're setting yourself up for disappointment. Why don't I get Ben to call Lawrence anyway?'

Meg hugged her friend fondly. Dear Tabby. She wanted to make the world in the shape she fancied. But Meg had no intention of partnering the bald and desperate Lawrence to the dance. 'Get your hat and a knife and fork ready to eat it with,' she said cheekily, letting Tabby go and waving as she went out the door.

* * *

Once Meg was back in the cottage, her happy confidence evaporated. Ben was babysitting for Katie, who was having an afternoon nap. She paid him despite his protests that he was glad to watch Katie for nothing, and he loped away back up to the fields to find Alex, the puppy at his heels. As much as she liked Primrose Cottage, it didn't feel as *normal* as Tabby's house. It was hard to know what she meant by that. Analysing it, Meg realised she felt vulnerable here in what was meant to be her secure home. When she was at Tabby's, it felt as if nothing horrible could ever happen. The Shaws had a normal, boisterous, large family with no dark shadows fringing it. By meeting Phillip and marrying him, Meg had brought darkness into her life. It was her own fault. She had fallen for his sophistication and good looks and his wealthy lifestyle. Not to mention the zeal with which he'd courted her and the layers of charm he'd expended to lure her in.

That was when it came to her. She was in danger of living her whole life in fear of him. She was being passive, waiting for him to do something. It couldn't go on. She felt anger rising in her. How dare he taunt her with his presence and his phone calls. It had to end. She was going to make him stop. And if he didn't, then she'd threaten to tell Leila what he was doing. Meg's heart began to beat fast and painfully in her chest. She swallowed nervously, but she was determined. She was going to go to Kew and confront Phillip.

\* \* \*

The Kew townhouse looked immaculate, expensive and uninviting behind its black railings. Meg had miraculously

138

managed to park right outside it. She left Katie strapped in her car seat, bribed with some sweeties and a new doll and colouring book. She carefully checked that the car was locked. There was no way she was taking her inside and she had no intention of staying long. She had no idea how Phillip was going to react to her impulsive visit. At the end of the short road there was a long queue of tourists waiting to get into the botanic gardens: a brightly coloured moving snake of chatter and maps. London was at the peak of its tourist season, and the wonderful green expanse of Kew Gardens was always a favourite with visitors.

She pushed open the gate with its spiked top. A lime-green Maserati was parked crossways on the slabbed driveway. She wondered if it was Phillip's or Leila's. It was quite a contrast to her own ancient Fiesta. The front garden was tiled, with no weeds or grass anywhere. A single fig tree grew in an enormous blue glazed pot. One curled brown leaf had dared to drop onto the terracotta surface in defiance of the householders. Strangely, it gave her the strength she needed to lift her hand and ring the bell.

Phillip didn't even raise an eyebrow when he motioned her to come in. It was as if he'd been expecting her. Meg took a long, measured, silent breath in and stepped onto the cream pile carpet. Inside, the house looked just as it had when she lived there. It was sparsely furnished but what furniture there was, was extremely expensive and in excellent taste. The style was predominantly black wood and steel. There was artwork tastefully hung on the walls — modern pieces with a few lines of colour or texture. It wasn't to Meg's liking. But then it never had been. When she married Phillip she imagined they'd work together to decorate their home. But it was always Phillip's house and he hadn't allowed her to change anything. Clearly, Leila hadn't had much more luck either. There wasn't a feminine touch anywhere.

'To what do I owe the honour?' Phillip asked mockingly.

'Let's not beat about the bush,' Meg replied, more confidently than she felt. 'I know what you're doing and I want you stop.'

'And what exactly is it that you think I'm doing?' Phillip strolled across the vast living room and leaned against the mantelpiece to watch her with hooded eyes.

'Phoning me at all hours of the night, for one thing,' she said.

'Phoning you? Have you any proof of that?' he asked mildly. He opened a slim tin on the mantelshelf, took out a cigarette and lit it. A curl of grey smoke snaked up. She'd always hated him smoking. She remembered begging him to stop, at first because she loved him and worried about his health, and later because she loved her baby and didn't want the smoke to affect Katie's health. But Phillip refused to give up. In fact, he had usually done the opposite of anything she'd wished him to do. Now she under-stood it was all part of his powerful need to be in control, but back then she had been confused and disappointed. She was even more glad she hadn't brought Katie into the house with her today.

'I know it's you. Just as I know it was you in that blue car last week up on the moors watching me.' Meg bunched her fists so tightly she heard her knuckle crack.

Phillip smiled at her and Meg shivered. It wasn't a nice smile. It was predatory, like the smile of a reptile. 'Dear, dear. I hope you aren't sharing these imaginings of yours with anyone. They might start to believe you're being paranoid. Why would I be watching you? I'm married to someone else and I have a business to run. It's most unlikely.'

Meg felt a flicker of uncertainty. Wasn't that what Tabby and Garth were gently implying too? Was she over-reacting? But his next words confirmed her fears.

'I would advise you not to tell your

gentleman friend about your accusations. Nobody wants to associate with a mad woman.'

'You couldn't possibly know about Garth unless you were in that car at the picnic spot, watching us. Are you going to deny it?'

Phillip gave a short bark of laughter. 'Deny it? Actually, why should I bother? No one's going to believe you, after all, and there's no one in the house to overhear us.'

As he walked towards her, Meg was utterly conscious of the silence and coldness of the house. He said there was no one else in the house and she was convinced. Leila must be out shopping or visiting friends, if Phillip allowed her any. She wondered fleetingly whether he treated his second wife the same way he'd treated her. Then he was right there, intimidating and tall, and invading her personal space. She could do nothing but step back to distance them, but she didn't want to give him that satisfaction of making her give way. So she held her ground and fixed him with a steady gaze.

'Are you a good mother, Meg?' Phillip whispered against her ear.

She felt the hot breath on her lobe, yet her body went cold at his words.

'I'm checking up on you. If I decide you're not doing a good job bringing up my daughter then I'll take her from you. You've been warned.'

With a cry of horror, Meg leapt away from him. She ran from the house, fumbling for her car keys and hardly able to see through her panic. The keys fell to the ground and into the gutter. She knelt, scrambling in the dirt, trying to pick them up and dreading that Phillip had followed her out and would grab Katie. She found the keys, scraping her nails dreadfully, and shakily unlocked the car. The house remained shut but she sensed him in there watching her. *Watching her*.

She turned the ignition, willing it to start first go. Then with a throaty roar of the engine, she took it too fast round the corner and out of sight of all her worst nightmares.

'Mummy, I want to go to the big park!' Katie cried, pointing to the lawns of Kew, visible behind the street railings. 'I want to go now!' Her legs kicked the back of Meg's seat and she pushed her body rigid in her restraint. She was working up to a tantrum.

'Stop it, you're a bad girl to whine,' Meg snapped, her nerves frayed beyond hope and distracted by Katie's sobs from the thick London traffic on the medieval-sized roads.

Katie burst into real crying at her mother's reprimand and Meg regretted her outburst immediately. She parked in a gap on the road, ignoring the loud blare of the horn from the outraged driver behind her, who swerved and gestured as he went past.

'I'm sorry. Mummy's sorry.' Meg clambered into the back seat and cuddled Katie tightly. 'I shouldn't have shouted at you, darling. It's not your fault. We'll go to the park when we get home, okay? Shall we ask Ben and his puppy to come too?'

Katie sniffed and wiped her nose on her wrist. The tears stopped at the mention of Ben and his dog and she affectionately pushed her face into Meg's neck. Meg felt her heart would break with the rush of love. A horrible thought struck her as she got back into the driver's seat and started the car once again. What if Phillip had seen her telling Katie off? What if he judged her on that and decided she wasn't a good mother? What if he came for Katie?

# 9

It was late into the night when she finally halted the car outside the cottage. The sky was clear and the Milky Way was a pale streak of endless stars, had she cared to look up. Meg hurried inside, carrying Katie, and bolted the door behind them. Once Katie was tucked up in bed she went downstairs and into the kitchen. She had made it a really cosy space with a blue and white polka dot tablecloth on the pine table, a matching blue china teapot on a ceramic stand and her collection of antique porcelain bowls displayed on Vinny's small Welsh dresser. Usually it gave her a lift of pleasure coming into this room, but now it made her want to cry. It was as if Phillip had the ability to drain all her happiness by his every action.

Meg shut the curtains. The black reflection from the glass made her uneasy. Anyone could be out there looking in, and she wouldn't know it. She ran the hot tap and filled the sink with washing-up liquid. She wiped the worktop surfaces and gave the cooker an unnecessary wash. The fact was that Phillip had never really gone away. She'd fled from him and thought herself safe and separate in a new phase of her life, but the truth was, he'd always been there in the background. He didn't want her — he'd made that quite clear — but he wasn't prepared to let her go, either. Not yet. Not until *he* wanted to. Meg, apparently, had no say in the matter.

Frustrated and angry, she flung open the fridge. She hadn't picked up any shopping that day and there was very little in it: a jar of mayonnaise, a box of eggs, a round of camembert and a bottle of white wine. She broke open the cap on the wine, glad she didn't have to search for a corkscrew, and poured a large glass. She took it to the kitchen table and sat down. A few large sips later she felt a warmth and calmness. She was quite hungry, but too tired to bother getting up again to make toast. There was a comforting low buzz from the fridge and it felt good to unwind with her wine in her lovely blue and white room. She'd put Phillip out of her mind. Tomorrow she might come up with a solution to her problems. It seemed easier the more she sat there.

The faint knocking crept slowly into her consciousness. Meg yawned and refilled her glass. There were often countryside noises at night. At first she'd flinched at every one of them, but once she discovered that trees creak, sheep cough and birds are capable of singing throughout the night, she didn't react. But the knocking came again, a little louder. Someone was at the front door. She wasn't scared. If it was Phillip, she'd knock him down! Emboldened by the alcohol, Meg got up and swayed dizzily. She caught the table corner for balance and went to the door.

Garth was there. He looked wonderfully handsome in his casual bush trousers and open-necked check shirt, and his eyes were even darker blue than she remembered. She had a strong urge to kiss him and run her hands through his thick hair. She stumbled on the lip of the doorstep and he caught her. 'What are you doing here?' she mumbled, smiling up at him.

Why was he frowning at her? She hadn't invited him in, that was it. How remiss of her.

'Come in, come in.' She waved vaguely, feeling faintly light-headed.

'I saw a light on and wondered if you were okay,' Garth said, still frowning at her. 'I couldn't sleep and I've been walking the fields. Is everything all right?'

Meg was surprised to find they were in the kitchen. She didn't remember getting there. There was the sound of breaking glass and she stared down at the broken shards of wine glass.

'Oops,' she giggled, then fell back into a chair.

'You're drunk,' Garth said. He sounded stern and Meg found that incredibly funny too.

'You need to sober up,' he went on.

With a switch of mood, she was then highly irritated with him. How dare he come visiting in the middle of the night and tell her what to do! If only her head wasn't pounding, she'd be able to tell him just what she thought. She tried anyway.

'I'm not drunk, thank you very much. I'm in my own house, minding my own business and having a little glass of wine. That's all. If you don't like it, then leave. I didn't ask you to come here.'

'I was worried about you.'

'Well you don't need to be. I'm perfectly capable of looking after myself.'

Garth gripped her arm firmly. 'Not right now you're not. How can you drink when Katie's up there asleep? It's irresponsible behaviour,' he muttered under his breath and released her.

Meg stared at him, the shock of his anger making her abruptly sober. He was right. She shouldn't be drinking when she was the only adult in the house. She never did drink more than a tiny half glass usually because of Katie. She felt sick and her head pounded.

'Here, drink this.' It was an order. A mug of hot black liquid appeared under her nose. Meg sipped it, wincing at the heat on her tongue. It was strong black coffee and it sharpened her senses and took away the soft blurry edges around her. She looked at Garth and groaned. He still looked angry with her. That was okay; she was angry with herself.

'Better?' he asked in a brusque tone, as if he didn't much like her at all.

'I don't normally drink this much,' she said defensively.

'Really?' he said with an edge of sarcasm that annoyed her.

'Yes, really. Do you think I'm lying? Of course I wouldn't drink when I'm in charge of Katie alone here.'

'People who drink heavily tend to be inveterate liars. Why should you be any different?' Garth's voice had a bitter edge to it.

The coffee had kicked in and Meg lost her nausea and headache. She'd only had two large glasses of wine in reality, and she had been more affected than she should've been because she wasn't used to it and because of her nervy exhaustion. But how to explain that to a furious Garth? Then she got it.

'This isn't about me, not really. Who is it? Was Anna a heavy drinker?'

She'd hit her target with a lucky shot. Garth sagged as if the air had gone from his lungs. 'Anna was an alcoholic. I had no idea when I married her that she had a problem. She drank secretly from an early age but she was clever at lying and deceiving her family and me, and able to function well despite her addiction.'

'I'm sorry, Garth. I didn't know,' Meg whispered.

'How could you know?' He shook his head. 'No one did. I found out after we'd been married a couple of years and she couldn't hide it anymore. We both wanted a baby and had been trying since we wed. When it didn't happen she became depressed and alcohol was her solace, not me.'

'How awful for both of you,' Meg said. She curled her fingers around his and moved unconsciously closer to him, as if she could draw out his sorrow and take it away.

'We got help and Anna seemed to making a good recovery,' Garth went on. 'I came to terms with the fact I wouldn't ever be a father and I thought Anna had made her peace with it too. We talked about the travel we could do as a couple that we wouldn't have managed with kids in tow. We spoke about how we'd be closer, just the two of us, without having to share our love. We made the future sound as good as it could. And I wanted it, just me and Anna. It was going to be marvellous.'

'But she didn't get well?' Meg guessed.

'She never gave up drinking. She hid it from me and lied about her recovery. She couldn't bear to see me unhappy, that's what she said when I finally found out. She did it for me. That was what hurt most of all. I was to blame.'

'But that's not true,' Meg cried. 'Surely she was to blame for her own mistakes. It wasn't fair to say it was your fault.'

'The night of the accident, we went to a party in the village,' Garth said, his voice almost breaking on the words as he forced them out. 'That was when I found out that she'd been lying to me all those months. I left her chatting to some other women and I went outside with a couple of my friends whom I hadn't seen in a while.

'Then there was a commotion and I was called inside by my friend's wife. Anna was sprawled on the bathroom floor. She was drunk and had fallen and chipped a tooth on the sink. It was all a terrible mess. I got her cleaned up and apologised to everyone. My friends helped me get her into the car. I tried not to see their pity or the relief in their faces that it wasn't *their* wife who was an embarrassing drunk. We headed home.'

'But you never got there.' Meg tightened her grip on his in horror at his unfolding story.

'We nearly did. I was driving, obviously. Anna was belligerent, as drunks get, and wanted to provoke an argument. Nothing I said calmed her down. She was raring for a fight. She accused me of not loving her, of only staying with her out of duty. She said terrible things. I tried to ignore her and made my mind up not to respond to her digs. I just wanted to get home safely and sober her up.

'The dog jumped out from the hedgerow right in front of the car. I would've missed it and there'd have been no accident if Anna hadn't at that very moment, in anger, wrenched the steering wheel from me. I don't know what she was doing, and I don't think she knew either, but the car went straight off the road and into the hedgerow, smack into an old beech tree.'

'And Anna was killed,' Meg finished rawly. No wonder Garth had hidden away at Winter Farm. What pain he must have suffered for four years on his own. The villagers' suspicions and the gossip had driven him further into his own company.

'What played on my mind afterwards is that Anna was right,' Garth said starkly. 'She accused me of falling out of love with her, and it was true. Her illness was so vast and absorbing that I lost the real Anna to it. The girl I knew when we were growing up together, the girl I fell in love with, ceased to exist once her drinking took control. When she was killed that night, my sorrow and my guilt were intensified by the knowledge that I hadn't loved her enough. Maybe the villagers were right to blame me. How did I manage to walk free from the wreckage with only a few lacerations and a broken arm?'

'No one can answer that,' Meg said. 'It wasn't your fault. You have to forgive yourself. If you don't, then how can you move on with your life? It's been four whole years.' She rose and filled two mugs with more coffee. She put them down on the table but neither of them took them. 'No wonder you got so angry seeing me tipsy,' she said. 'I'm sorry.'

'I shouldn't have reacted so badly,' Garth replied. 'Having a few glasses of wine hardly makes you an alcoholic. I should be apologising to you.'

'You don't need to do that. The wine was a reaction to the events of the day. I went to see Phillip.'

'What happened?' He looked at her with concern.

Meg smiled grimly. 'It was probably a bad idea, but I wanted to challenge him and tell him to leave me alone.'

'I'd have gone with you, if you'd asked.'

She knew he would have. She'd come to rely on his quiet strength and friendship. But was it only friendship that she felt? Hadn't it deepened into something quite different, if she was honest? She knew how he felt about her. All she had to do was say yes. Would Phillip leave her and Katie alone if she was together with Garth?

But that wasn't being fair to him. If she gave in to her attraction for him and her growing feelings, then it had to be for the right reasons. It had to be because she loved him. And right now it was all confused in her emotions with wanting to be rid of Phillip and his threats. Besides, until she sorted that out, wasn't she also putting Garth in danger?

Meg sighed. It was too complicated.

'Meg? Did Phillip agree to stop bothering you?' Garth asked insistently.

'Not exactly.' She told him all that had gone on in the Kew townhouse. 'He's very clever,' she finished up. 'There's no shred of evidence that he's stalking me and nothing I can take to the police. Phillip's very plausible and very charming. Besides, he socialises with the chief of police, or used to at any rate.'

'You and Katie should come and stay with me at the farm for a while,' Garth said.

'Do you think that's wise?' Meg released his fingers and felt cold without them. 'People might talk.'

'People talk anyway,' he said cryptically, and sighed. 'Perhaps you're right. But I'll be keeping a close watch over you in case Phillip comes back. I suspect he likes tormenting you but won't actually do anything. Hopefully he'll get bored with his games and leave you in peace.'

Meg wasn't so sure, but she didn't argue. He stroked the hair from her face tenderly and kissed her forehead. 'You should get to bed,' he said. 'It's almost three in the morning.'

She longed to melt into his warm embrace. It felt safe and strong and protective. But even touching her cheek to his in what was meant to be an equally friendly goodnight was suddenly dangerous. A surging heat rose in her body and the air pulsed between them. She felt the bristles on his jaw and smelt the clean male scent of him. His mouth brushed her skin so softly and she moaned.

With a ragged breath, Garth leapt up and put a distance between them. 'Good night, Meg. Sleep tight. Lock up well.' Without a further glance he left, shutting the front door quietly. She padded after him on bare feet and rose on tiptoe to bolt the locks. She laid her hot cheek against the cold painted wood and let her held breath out.

She couldn't sleep. Her body was vibrant with tingling nerve endings and she played over the sensation of Garth's skin touching hers. She couldn't deny it. She wanted him badly — so badly it was like an ache that had to be soothed.

She went into the living room and switched on her laptop. Getting some work done would dampen her desires and focus her mind. She opened her paper files and spread the sheets out on the sofa beside her. The words jiggled on the pages like hieroglyphics. She couldn't concentrate. She didn't even think about Phillip. All she saw was Garth, with his broad shoulders and firm jaw and oh-so-desirable body; and his kindness, his concern for her and his easy friendship.

She rubbed her face hard to dispel the images. *Focus, Meg. Write the article you were commissioned to do last week and haven't even started.* Fix the pile of paperwork and whittle it down in the hours of darkness remaining. She tried to write the first paragraph and then flung the paper and pen away from her in disgust.

It was no good. She couldn't work when all she could see in front of her was Garth Winter. Whether it was right or not, she couldn't stop it happening. It was like the break in a dam letting water pour through until it became a veritable flood. Whether she wanted to or not, Meg was in serious danger of falling in love with him.

# 10

The supermarket was busy with mothers and preschool children, tourists and older couples. Meg groaned at the sight of the queues at the checkout. Her trolley was piled high with all the essentials they had run out of. She was determined not to have to drive back into the large town for a few weeks. If she bought all her tins, packages and frozen goods in one big swoop, then they could get by with Burley's corner shop for milk and bread.

She took out her mobile phone, hesitated, then returned it to her handbag. No, she wouldn't phone. Katie was on a trial play day at a local nursery school and Meg was nervously praying that her daughter was happy. The woman in charge of the newbies' class had promised to phone her if there were any signs of tears. So far her phone had remained silent. Katie was proud to be going to school, just as Jane and Ellen were that day, the schools having now returned from the summer break. Going to nursery proved what a big girl she was.

Meg managed to get through the checkout fairly quickly and pushed her laden trolley to the boot of her car to fill it with bags. She had hours before she had to collect Katie. Enough time to put the shopping away in the cupboards and reward herself with a generous pot of tea before getting down to writing her latest commission. There was a sense of liberty in being on her own and it struck her that if Katie settled well at nursery three days a week, she'd get through her own work an awful lot faster. More work meant more money coming in. She might even be able to plan for a short holiday for the two of them in the spring.

She was humming a tune and deliberating on the merits of camping in France versus a weekend back in

London when she saw the sleek blue car parked outside her home. It looked familiar. She frowned and parked behind it as it was taking up her space. What a bother; now she'd have to trail her groceries just that bit further. Why did she recognise it?

As she got out, a slender woman got out of the blue car ahead of her. She was wearing a cream silk dress and linen jacket, with a bag slung over her shoulder casually and her sunglasses perched on a head of glossy curls pinned into a loose French plait. She had a coffee-and-cream complexion and everything about her screamed money. It was Leila Graham. Meg recognised her from the celebrity magazines; especially the one that had had the exclusive photos of Phillip and Leila's high-profile wedding.

Meg stood awkwardly, a large plastic shopping bag weighing her down on each side while Leila moved gracefully forward, her hand outstretched in greeting. Meg hastily dropped a bag to shake. Leila's grasp was cool and firm and her nails beautifully polished. A delicate flowery perfume exuded from her.

'Hello, Meg. We haven't met but I feel as if I know you. I'm Leila, Phillip's . . . wife.'

'Pleased to meet you,' Meg said. 'Would you like to come in?'

She opened the door, conscious of the woman following her. Thankfully she'd left the cottage relatively tidy. It shouldn't matter, but she didn't want Leila thinking badly of her.

'A cup of tea?' she offered, once her guest was sitting in the front room.

'No thank you. I won't stay long and I don't want to intrude on your day.' Leila's accent was smooth and rich like her looks.

'How did you know where I live?' Meg asked. *And why visit me now, when you've known about me for all the months of your marriage?*

'Isn't it obvious? Phillip left it written down on the message pad beside our telephone. He didn't even bother to try to hide it from me,' Leila said with an unhappy smile.

Meg saw that there were tiny lines around her mouth which weren't disguised by expensive face powder or distracted from by designer lip stain. Lines of strain or unhappiness. Life with Phillip clearly wasn't what Leila had hoped for either. So why was she here?

'I'm leaving him, you know. He doesn't realise it yet but after I leave here today, I'm not going back. My father's got a private jet and I'm taking it to my retreat in the Bahamas. One private place Phillip hasn't got his greedy grasp on.' Leila took her sunglasses off and stared at them as if they held all the answers. She sniffed and dabbed her nose with a tiny scrap of lace handkerchief and put it back in her oversized Gucci bag. 'Perhaps I will have that cup of tea after all, thank you, Meg.'

Meg was glad of a moment to gather her thoughts. She poured the boiling water onto a couple of teabags, saying a silent thanks that she had bought a box of them, and reached for the cups. When she got back to the living room, Leila was composed and her makeup retouched and perfect. Meg could see why Phillip had fallen for her. She was flawlessly beautiful and could easily have made her fortune in the fashion business. He'd be the envy of any other man with Leila at his side. He hadn't lost out when Meg ran away. He'd simply upgraded to a better model.

'I'm sorry your marriage has broken down, but why come here?' Meg asked. 'We don't know each other.'

'But we both know Phillip, don't we. We both know what he's like. When I saw your address written down beside the telephone, I wondered . . . I wondered whether there was something going on between you. Everything was marvellous for the first few months of our marriage,' Leila went on without waiting for Meg's response. 'I'm sure you can understand that. He's a charming, intriguing partner and, well, it's the little touches, isn't it, like roses on the pillow and love notes and chocolates. And Phillip did that in abundance.'

Meg remembered that. It had touched her that he was so thoughtful and romantic. Often a new dress would appear in her wardrobe and he wanted her to wear it to a particular function or party. It was a fairytale existence for the girl from a small northern town and lower-middle-class background.

'But then he started taking me for granted. He became irritable and we had so many arguments. He wanted me to stay in every night with him or only go to functions he went to. I told him quite plainly that I refused to do that, which made him very unhappy.'

So Phillip hadn't had it all his own way living with Leila. Meg had been an easier person to control. She hadn't had the backup of rich, important parents and hadn't been born with the sense of entitlement that wealthy families inherited along with blue eyes or dimpled chins.

'My marriage hasn't been working for quite a while,' Leila said sadly, 'which is why when I saw your name and address, I put two and two together and thought Phillip regretted divorcing you after all. But I was wrong — I can see it in your face, Meg. That's not why he's got in touch with you.'

'I'm really sorry your marriage has ended so badly,' Meg said, and she meant it. There was something likeable about Leila. In a different place and situation they might have been friends. 'But it isn't you, it's him. Phillip is a difficult man to live with and that's putting it mildly. I've discovered recently that he's been keeping tabs on me; where I live and what I do. I don't know why exactly, but I went to your house and asked him to stop.'

Leila looked shocked. 'I had no idea. I know he has a private detective on his payroll and uses him to keep track of business associates. Whether that's legal or not, I've no idea, and any time I queried his work practices he froze me out. But to have you followed and investigated, that's outrageous.'

'I thought so too,' Meg said with ironic humour, 'but that's not what has me most unsettled. It's Katie, my daughter. He never wanted her or showed any interest in her when she was born. But now he's threatening to take her from me.'

'That fits in with what he's been saying recently. In fact it was the last straw for me. He wanted us to start a family. But he knows I've never wanted to be a mother. He knew that when we got married and he told me then he didn't want children either. Now it's all he can talk about. He told me he's reached an age where he wants an heir to all his wealth. I put it down to a middle-age crisis, but it's persisted. I think you need to be very careful with Katie.'

Meg frowned. 'I should be glad that he's finally showing an interest in her. I've wished for it long enough. It's the way he's going about it. I'd be quite happy to discuss joint custody or visiting rights.'

Leila jumped up. 'That won't be enough for Phillip. When he wants something, he wants to own the whole of it. He'll never be satisfied with sharing your daughter, Meg. He'll want her all to himself.'

A chill went through Meg's body at Leila's words. Was she right? Couldn't Meg and Phillip come to some sort of mature agreement about their child? She was prepared to share Katie with him so that her daughter could have a relationship with her father. Surely Phillip wouldn't want to deny Katie her mother?

Leila glanced at her watch. 'I have to go. My pilot will be waiting for me.' She picked up her bag and put on her sunglasses. 'Take care, Meg. And keep your daughter close.'

As she watched Leila drive away, Meg remembered where she'd seen the car before. It was the blue car that had followed them on the moor. Phillip had borrowed Leila's car to watch her from.

Her instinct was to go to the nursery and take Katie away immediately. She even had the car keys in her hand before she realised she was being silly. If she went and demanded that Katie leave, she'd only distress everyone. Katie would be upset at having to go and the nursery staff would want to know why. Besides, she couldn't imagine even Phillip having the bravado to kidnap a child in broad daylight from a nursery class.

*Calm down. Keep a sense of proportion.* Phillip wasn't the bogeyman. He wasn't everywhere all at once. Yet she couldn't concentrate on her work. She went outside into the back garden. Before she knew it, she found herself at Garth's house. He was there, sitting at a large easel on his patio, paintbrush working furiously. When he saw her, he put it down and came to her.

As soon as she was enveloped in his embrace, Meg knew she was in love with him. She couldn't help it. It was visceral and all-encompassing. With him, she was home. Her heart lay with him. She reached up and kissed him fiercely. He returned it with equal vigour and she felt his heart beat on top of hers through the thin cotton of her blouse.

'I love you,' she whispered.

'I've waited for you to say that,' Garth replied. 'I love you too.' His kisses deepened in urgency and his body was hard against hers. His fingers stroked the back of her neck. She slid her hand up inside his shirt, feeling the taut muscles of his back and the heat of his skin. She moaned softly as he left a trail of kisses along her neck and down her collarbone to the swell of her breasts.

Garth led her inside and upstairs. He stopped momentarily and questioned her with his gaze. Meg nodded wordlessly and followed him into the bedroom.

# 11

'How can you be so certain that he'll turn up?' Tabby teased as she balanced one Tupperware container on top of another, the weight of the sponge cakes helping to keep them from spilling across the floor. 'Oh, did I mention that Lawrence is coming along today in any case?'

'Garth will be there,' Meg said with a grin, picking up a cool box full of salads.

'We'll see, won't we? Anyway, we'd better get this load of food over to the village green before Maurice phones again. He sounds flustered and the barbecue isn't even lit yet. Where are the kids?'

Meg hadn't told Tabby about her feelings for Garth yet. It was too new and wondrous and she wanted to hug it to herself for a little while longer. When she wasn't with him, she longed for him. She found herself humming tunes while she did the housework or cooked the meals. The world was a brighter, shinier place.

Garth wanted her and Katie to move up to Winter Farm to be with him. Meg was in two minds. It was too sudden and she had to think about it, she'd told him when he assumed that's what she'd do. It made a kind of sense, she admitted. They loved each other and wanted to be together. They hadn't discussed marriage but the assumption was there that they would do that in due course. It was just that Primrose Cottage had been her home for such a short while, and she loved it. It was odd to imagine not living there. Also, she'd uprooted Katie from Tottenham so recently, and now she would be asking her to uproot again from another home. Was that fair? Was it too confusing for a three-year-old? Garth told her to take all the time she needed. There was no pressure on her to move immediately, but he hoped they would soon.

'Ellen! Get your brothers to come down here and lift this stuff for me,' Tabby bellowed up the stairs. 'Come on Meg, we're not waiting for that lot. They know where to come to. Where's Katie?'

'Ben's bringing Katie down to the green,' Meg told her. 'I can't separate her from Poppy the puppy, and Poppy is devoted to Ben, so the three of them come as a package at the moment. I can't bear to think what'll happen with Katie if Ben goes.'

'Has he made any contact with his family?' Tabby asked as they walked along the pavement with their laden bags.

'Up until yesterday the answer to that would've been no, but he told me this morning that he phoned his mother last night. Garth was really pleased with him for doing it and I could see that Ben was glad to earn Garth's approval.' Meg smiled. 'They're good for each other, you know, Tabby. Ben needs a father figure to guide him and Garth's needed company. Ben's so keen on farming that it's given Garth a renewed interest in Winter Farm. Alex is happier, too, now that Garth's taking more responsibility.'

'Sounds like you know an awful lot about the goings-on at Winter Farm,' Tabby remarked shrewdly. She treated Meg to one of her hard stares. Meg blushed.

'So I think that Ben's mother might be coming to the barbecue today,' she went on quickly. 'It's neutral ground for them to meet on.'

'What on earth went on at his home for him to run away?' Tabby said, shaking her head. 'I can't imagine any of my lot running off. If they did, they'd soon be back for dinner and to get their washing done.'

'But you and Maurice have provided such a warm, loving home for them,' Meg said. 'Sometimes I've wished I could move in too.'

Tabby laughed, 'If I wasn't carrying

these blasted bags, I'd give you a big hug. You can move in any time. I'd love an extra pair of hands to cook the dinners and iron the school clothes.'

'Oh well, if that's the deal then no thanks,' Meg joked. 'I've got enough of that at the cottage.'

'Seriously though, why did Ben leave?'

Meg shrugged. 'He hasn't laid it out in much detail, but just said that he wasn't wanted. Reading between the lines, I'd say there's a new stepfather and stepsister, and like all new joined families there needs to be a settling-in phase. Ben clearly didn't wait about for that. I hope he can resolve his issues today with his mother.'

Meg thought about Garth and Katie. If she did move up to the farm, she couldn't envisage a long settling period for them. Katie was very fond of Garth and the feeling was mutual.

'Well, good luck to them both,' Tabby said heartily. 'Here we go, dump those there on that table and I'll give this

Tupperware to Norah, who's in charge of the home baking.'

The village green was a square of open mown grass in the middle of Burley village. It was surrounded by the old church and its attendant hall on one side, a row of shops on two sides, and the cobbled road down to the beach on the last. There was coloured bunting strung between the lamp-posts and a long line of trestle tables covered in red paper tablecloths and white paper party plates. There were plastic drinking cups and plastic cutlery being laid out by three small girls and a slim, brown-haired woman was folding napkins and passing them to a boy who carefully put one at each place.

Beyond the trestles, the barbecue was in the process of being lovingly filled with coals and slowly heated by a group of men. Meg recognised Maurice's tall, thin back bent over the grills. Jacob and William arrived and ran over to join the male ritual of lighting and tending the barbecue. The doors to the church hall were wide open and the sound of country music being practiced by violins came wafting out. A group of women laughing and chatting spilled out of the hall and advanced towards the tables.

A car horn tooted and they all waved and shouted like mad as another family emerged from the car to join the growing throng.

'It gets pretty busy,' Tabby said, smiling, as she joined Meg again. 'Right, let's see what has to be done. Where's Norah got to? Can you see if you can find Bethany and ask her whether the wine boxes have arrived yet? She's the one with the red hair in a ponytail over there.'

Meg lost Tabby to the other women and left her giving orders and shouting at her children. William's T-shirt was striped with coal dust where fingers had been wiped, and Jacob was kicking a football dangerously close to all the activities. Ellen and her friends, never separated, were helping the brown-haired mother, and Ellen didn't even look up at her own mother's yelling, but went on placidly pouring juice into large jugs held solemnly by a little round-faced girl with blonde pigtails and blue-framed glasses.

After passing on Tabby's message to a harassed Bethany, Meg wandered over to peer into the church hall. There was more bunting along the walls and over the ancient stage at the back of the hall. The place smelt like any church hall she'd ever been in: a mixture of damp mould, old plaster and waxed linoleum floors. This was overlaid by warm summer air and the chalk from the violins' string bows. Up on the stage, back-dropped by the curling, faded posters of last year's musical production, were four musicians practising their dance melodies. Every few bars they stopped and one of them munched on a sandwich in snatched mouthfuls.

'Meg!'

She turned to find Ben and Katie and Poppy.

'Mummy, look. Poppy chases a ball.

Look.' Katie hunkered down and Poppy sat suddenly the way a puppy does. A soggy tennis ball dropped from her mouth and her tongue lolled out of her pink mouth as she cocked a silky soft ear at the little girl. Katie took the ball and threw it onto the grass. The puppy shot off and got it and brought it back, panting in excitement.

'See, Mummy? She did it,' Katie said proudly.

'That's great, darling,' Meg said. 'You promised me you'd stick closely with Ben today, remember?'

'I will, I promise.' Katie nodded seriously, but her eyes were for Poppy only.

Meg had told Garth and Ben about her fears over Phillip taking Katie. She said she thought it unlikely, but just in case she didn't want Katie wandering about on her own at the barbecue. Ben promised to keep an eye on her.

'Ben, when your mother arrives, let me know and I'll take Katie and give you two some privacy,' Meg said.

'I'll bring Katie over to you,' Ben agreed, 'if Mum does turn up.' He sounded so young and unsure that Meg's heart went out to him.

'Of course she'll turn up,' she said. 'She's your mother. She must be missing you so much.'

His mouth gave a little twist but he didn't say more about it. Taking Katie by the hand and Poppy by the lead, he took his companions over in the direction of the game of football that had grown into a team of most of the village children. The players were being directed into the nearby street to play. There was no danger of cars as the adjacent streets had been blocked off to traffic.

Meg noticed that the place was filling up fast. It wasn't just villagers, but nearby townsfolk and tourists who came along, Tabby had told her. On a dry, hot day there could be hundreds of people milling about the green and the nearby streets and lanes. The sky was azure blue and the sun a round yellow orb casting a heat that was beginning to scorch the top of Meg's head. There was no rain forecast so Tabby reckoned this year's barbecue and dance would be swelled out with record numbers of people.

But where was Garth? She heard the band strike up the notes for the first dance and the compere's voice over a crackly microphone welcoming everybody and asking them to grab a partner for the first waltz.

'Ah, there you are.' Tabby grabbed her arm. 'We'd better hurry.'

'Hurry? What for?'

'The first dance. Miraculously, Maurice has left the barbecue in order to dance with me. Will wonders never cease? Where's Garth? Never mind; Lawrence is over there. Come on, Meg!'

Meg found herself dragged along in Tabby's enthusiastic wake. She was introduced to Lawrence through the loud noise of what seemed like hundreds of feet slapping on the church hall's floor and the scrape and zing of the violins in an age-old country tune. Lawrence had clammy hands and a shiny, eager face as he moved Meg round the dance floor with more vigour than talent.

She caught Tabby's wink of encouragement as Maurice swirled his wife around, and gave her a weak smile. Lawrence leaned in to ask her if she came to dance here often and there was a whiff of his stale breath. She felt a twinge of doubt about Garth. Had he changed his mind about his feelings for her? Where was he, for goodness sake? He'd promised to be here. He hadn't hesitated when she'd asked. He'd only joked that he was ready to come out of hiding and show his face to the village. Maybe he was having second thoughts. After all, from what Tabby had said, people here had been vicious in their gossip about him and Anna. Meg should never have arrived separately. She should go and find him. If only Lawrence didn't have such a tight grip on her elbows. He knocked her knee with his as they danced and apologised profusely. Poor Lawrence. It wasn't his fault she didn't find him at all attractive and that she was deeply in love with another man. She rubbed her throbbing knee and stopped dancing.

'This won't do, we have to keep up with the music,' Lawrence said, trying to pull her up and along.

'May I borrow your partner for the rest of this dance?' a deep, familiar voice asked.

'No, you certainly cannot,' Lawrence replied tetchily with a high-pitched indignant squeak. 'Find your own partner. Meg's my date.'

Garth raised an eyebrow and Meg smothered a smile. He was gorgeous in a sky-blue brushed cotton shirt and grey casual trousers, and her pulse rate increased at the mere sight of him.

'I'm sorry, Lawrence, but I did promise Garth a dance,' she said, trying to hide her relief as she slipped into Garth's arms.

'He's got a nerve showing up here,' Lawrence muttered, stomping off. Meg was going to feel sorry for him but his final remark took the wind from her lungs. Garth stiffened but she kept dancing and he had to go with her.

'Ignore him,' she said sharply. 'It's his wounded pride talking. He knows nothing about you.'

'He's only voicing what a lot of others will be thinking. Anyway, I'm sorry I'm late, but there was a sheep caught in the barbed wire in the top field and Alex and I had to free it.'

The dance came to an end and everybody clapped. Men were mopping sweating brows and women fanned themselves. It was getting hotter in the hall with all the bodies and energy of the dances. The music started up once more and Meg grabbed Garth for a foxtrot. There were curious glances as local people realised Garth Winter was amongst them. With determination, Meg ignored them and laughed and chatted in Garth's ear so that he wouldn't notice them.

'I know what you're doing and I love

you for it,' Garth said when the foxtrot ended and they queued for drinks. 'But perhaps I shouldn't have come down.'

'Nonsense,' Tabby interjected, over-hearing him. 'It's lovely to see you socialising here and nobody's going to say a word about anything. Trust me.' Tabby was very popular in the village and her word held a lot of sway. Meg knew if Tabby acted a certain way, most of the other women would follow suit.

'Why don't you two join us for drinks over at the barbecue?' Tabby said firmly. 'Maurice needs to cook the steaks and whatnot, and there's always room for more male advice.' She hooked her arm into Garth's as she spoke and steered him away. Maurice shrugged at Meg.

'My wife has it under control as usual,' he said mildly. 'We'd better follow on like good little soldiers. Besides, there's a queue for charred sausages already.'

There was a circle of families at the barbecue, some helping to cook and serve food and others there simply to talk to each other. There was a tiny pause in the conversation as Garth and Meg joined the crowd. Tabby talked loudly and cheerfully to Garth about his paintings, insisting she wanted to buy one. The group seemed to collectively relax and the murmur of conversation began again.

Meg hadn't realised she was holding her breath until it came out in one long gush. Tabby pushed a long, cold drink of cranberry juice at her and winked. Garth appeared from the grey smoke of the grills with a similar glass and grinned at her.

'I owe Tabby for that,' he said in a low tone. 'She's made it quite clear that I'm to be welcomed.'

'And why ever not?' Meg said indignantly. 'It was never your fault. You shouldn't have been banished to the farm.'

'I banished myself to brood over the accident and to come to terms with Anna's death,' Garth reminded her. 'But that's over now. I hope Anna will forgive me for letting her go and for moving on.'

'Of course she will. You've given her four years of mourning. That's sufficient. You've got your whole life ahead of you.'

'And a special, beautiful woman to share it with.'

Meg heard the faint question in Garth's remark. She had to tell him. It was only fair. She'd thought long and hard about whether to move from Primrose Cottage to Winter Farm to make a life with him since he'd asked about it. She'd weighed up her own feelings and how she thought Katie would respond, and all the other considerations large and small.

'Yes, I do want to share life with you. I was going to tell you today, that Katie and I will be moving up the hill to join you at Winter Farm.'

Regardless of people around them, he gathered her in his arms and kissed her with barely suppressed passion. Lawrence, hovering on the edge of the group, scowled and looked away.

'Thank you, Meg. Thank you.'

Garth's voice shook with emotion.

'It's me who should thank you for giving me a chance to love again,' Meg said shakily. She wiped away a tear.

'Is that a happy one?' Garth teased, seeing her mop her eye. He crushed her to him and they laughed together. She'd never felt so happy, so *whole*.

'Wait here,' he said suddenly. 'I've got something for you. But I've left it in the car. I didn't know if this was the right day to give it to you. But yes, it is.'

Meg sat at one of the long wooden benches and hummed a little tune. She wondered what he was going to get for her. Bethany came along with a tray of sausage rolls and offered her some. She picked at them, not really hungry as she was so full of love. She sipped the cranberry drink, marvelling how delicious it was with a twist of lemon and a couple of ice cubes.

She scanned the crowds for Ben and Katie. There they were, with Ellen, Jacob, William and a bunch of other kids. The boys were still kicking a football about against the kerb of the street while the girls had moved on to hula-hoops. Poppy was jumping up to chew on Katie's hoop while Ben leaned against the wall, keeping watch and talking to someone on his new mobile phone. Garth had bought it for him and insisted he could only keep it if he contacted his parents. That threat had worked well. Meg decided it was probably his mother phoning him to arrange a place to meet. Soon she'd have to go over and get Katie. Ben needed space with his mother on his own.

She half rose from the bench, thinking she'd go and ask Ben when his mother was arriving, when she saw him: a tall man, his back to her, weaving through the crowds. He was at least half a foot taller than most of the people round about him and he was wearing a white Panama hat with a black band. It was Phillip. She couldn't see his face but she didn't need to. She was certain it was him. The man had the same gait she'd glimpsed that long-ago day on the

Tottenham Court Road. A confident swagger. A way of walking that said he was important compared to the swarm around him.

Meg froze in indecision. Should she grab Katie? Or should she go after Phillip and challenge him? She looked over at the street. Katie was surrounded by a gang of kids. She was safe there. She looked along the road where Phillip was walking away. If she didn't run after him now she'd lose him. Where was he going in any case? It was as if he'd arrived at the green and looked it over and was now sauntering around the village. What was he up to?

There was only one thing to do, and that was to talk to him and find out. She hurried away from the green, vaguely aware of Tabby's querying call behind her. With many apologies and 'excuse me's she squeezed between people and followed the progress of the Panama hat.

Meg cursed the fact that she was so small and slight. She had to stop and rise up on tiptoe every few steps to see him. Once he turned back and with a curl of dread, she saw it was indeed Phillip. She had held a small flicker of hope that it was all in her imagination and that it was another tall man out for a day of sunshine, dancing and nice food. But it was her ex-husband. Out and about in a village he had no reason to visit other than that Meg and Katie had moved here to escape him.

Had he seen her? She doubted it, but then a few steps on when she again peered up and out of the heads to find him, the hat had gone. With a cry of frustration she surged on. Someone elbowed her in the side painfully as she pushed through the families and another person stood heedlessly on her foot.

Eventually she stopped, exhausted, at the end of a lane well away from the village green. The side street led down to the beach, and the other street she guessed led out of the village towards the main road, but she wasn't sure of its orientation. All she knew was she'd lost

Phillip. There were fewer people here and he couldn't hide in a crowd. But he'd gone all the same. She was limping because of the stomp on the top of her foot and she felt hot and sweaty and slightly unwell. Her heart was racing too fast in her ribcage, as if she was coming down with a virus.

There was nothing to be done except retrace her steps back to the green. With any luck Phillip had gone home. He must have seen how secure Katie was. She shivered to think he might have been watching her and Garth dancing or kissing or chatting at the barbecue. Why couldn't he leave her alone? What had Leila leaving him done to his state of mind? If she knew Phillip, then it would've made him absolutely livid to be abandoned by a second wife. To be out of control of what was happening in his life would be anathema to him. He'd want to regain control. And how better to do that than by manipulating Meg, who was such easy prey?

But what he didn't know was that Meg was stronger now. She was no longer on her own. She had Garth and Ben and Tabby and Maurice and the children. Straightening up, she went back as quickly as possible, the limp delaying her as she slipped through the people in the opposite direction.

'Meg, where did you go?' Garth rose to meet her with concern. He held a brown paper-wrapped package.

'I . . . went for a little walk,' she said. 'Is that your surprise for me?'

She should have told him about Phillip. But Phillip was gone, she was sure of that. He hadn't done any harm and she wanted to put it out of her mind. There was a desperate desire in her to cling to the happiness and *ordinariness* of the day. If she told Garth what had happened, he'd only worry and insist they call the police. He'd told her when she last raised her fears about Phillip that they had to involve the authorities if he got in touch again, even if they had no proof of what he was doing. But Meg didn't believe that was the answer. Phillip was too smart and he knew too many high-ranking people. Besides, he was still Katie's father for better or for worse.

'It's a small gift,' Garth said, giving it to her but still frowning. 'Is everything okay? Are you limping?'

'Someone stood on my foot,' she said truthfully. 'Can I open this?' She tore off the paper carefully to find a gilt-framed oil painting of Primrose Cottage. 'Oh Garth, it's beautiful,' she whispered. 'Thank you.'

'I thought that if you have to leave Vinny's cottage to live with me, then you'd like a daily reminder of it.'

But there was yelling in the background, a commotion that was barrelling their way. Then Ben was standing in front of them and Meg saw his mouth moving, but she couldn't hear the words. She didn't want to hear them. He was red with heat and sweat and panic and he was shouting at her frantically.

'Katie's vanished! I can't find her! She's gone!'

# 12

'Phillip was right here?'

And she hadn't trusted him enough to tell him. Garth stared at Meg. She sank down onto the bench, her face white and her large grey eyes beseeching him. Beside him, Ben was gabbling away agitatedly, and Garth realised there was a thin older woman with long white-streaked hair too.

'I'm so sorry, Meg,' Ben was saying, his words tumbling out. 'I only took my eyes off her for a moment. My mum arrived and I was looking for you so you could take Katie, but I couldn't find you, and then when I looked back she'd gone. How could it happen so quickly? I don't understand it.'

Ben's mother stared at all of them as if she didn't understand a word of what was going on. Garth didn't blame her. How could any of this have occurred?

'It's not your fault. It's mine. I shouldn't have left Katie with you. She should've been with me.' Meg tried to smile reassuringly at Ben but her mouth wobbled.

'If it was Phillip who took her then we can intercept him, if we move fast,' Garth said urgently. 'He can't have come on foot. What kind of car does he drive?'

His question galvanized Meg. She stood up and clutched at him. 'Yes, you're right. We can go after him if we're fast. He has a green Maserati. He won't have Leila's blue car, since she took it with her. Come on, let's go.'

'I'm parked at the edge of Burley in the public car park,' Garth told her.

They moved as fast as possible through the happy families on the green eating hot dogs and sausages in buns. The smell of sizzling meat and ketchup and mustard was cloying. He felt a nausea rise up in his throat. He was very fond of Katie. He loved her mother and Katie was the daughter he'd never had. If Phillip harmed her in any way . . . But he was her natural father, and from what Meg was telling him as they ran to the car park, he wanted Katie all to himself, to bring up without her mother.

'Why didn't you tell me about Leila's visit to you? Why didn't you say you'd seen Phillip at the barbecue today?'

Meg shook her head helplessly. There was no opportunity to hear her answers anyway as they reached Garth's car. He unlocked it quickly and threw the passenger door lock for her. His battered old car was no match for a sports car like Phillip's, but it was all they had and it would have to do.

'Where will he go? Think, Meg. You know him better than anyone. Try to put yourself in his shoes. He's taken Katie and now he'll want to lie low for a while. I'll phone the police while you decide which route we should take.'

To his surprise, she stilled his arm as he reached for his mobile. 'No, don't call the police, please.'

'Why not? He's kidnapped a child. We must get the authorities involved right now.'

'Please, Garth, let's do this ourselves,' Meg begged. 'He's still Katie's father. I don't know what's going through his mind right now, but I can't call the police on him. Not yet. Not until I've had the chance to talk to him. I just want my little girl back.'

Garth nodded grimly. It was Meg's decision to make. A gulf of some sort had opened up between them. He didn't know if Meg felt it too. But he felt as if he had no right to make any decisions on this. He wasn't part of this and he had no rights. He wasn't Meg's husband and he wasn't Katie's father. He could only help as far as he was allowed. But that didn't mean he wouldn't do his utmost to get Meg's child back for her. Afterwards they would have to sort it out.

'When I saw him, Phillip was walking away from the green as if he'd been there and seen what he needed to see.

He was walking quite purposefully in the opposite direction.'

'So he'd have seen you and me at the barbecue,' Garth said, 'and possibly he'd have seen Katie with the other kids in the street next to it. So where was he headed?'

'I think he was going back to his car. He could easily access the street where the children were playing from the other side of Burley.'

'But how did he manage to get Katie when she was in the midst of the children and Ben was there too? It doesn't make any sense. Are we off on a wild goose chase? Is she simply lost in the village?' Garth had started driving while they spoke but he braked then. They were assuming Phillip had taken Katie. But there were other more innocent explanations. She was only three years old. Toddlers wandered off.

'No. I know he's got her.' Meg's voice was strained but steady. 'And I know where he's going. Turn left up here.'

Garth did as she commanded and

the car wheels spun too fast as they took the curve. The engine whined but he had control and the car rocketed forward on the empty country road.

'There's no way he's going home to the house in Kew,' Meg said. 'It's too easy for us to follow him there. But there's a summer house in Hove that I'd almost forgotten about. He took me there when we first got married. It's right on the beach, a white house near the lagoons.'

'Are you certain?'

'It's the only place I can think of. He might have other properties that I don't know about. But Hove's only a couple of hours away along the coastal road. He could hole up there until he decides what to do next. Can't you go any faster?'

The car was hurtling fast as it could, with traffic mercifully light. To their right the sea glistened brightly and to their left the car windows were brushed with vegetation from high hedgerows. Blocks of houses came and went and the coastal road twisted and snaked, leaving the beaches and returning as it wound through settlements and avoided the cliffs.

'There he is!' Meg shouted, pointing ahead of them.

Garth saw a flash of virulent lime green as a sports car crested the hill stretch and disappeared over it. Phillip was clearly so confident no one was after him that he was cruising along like a tourist on a day outing.

'The trouble is that he'll recognise this car from our day on the moors,' Garth said. 'If he sees us and speeds up, we'll never catch him.'

'Then we go to Hove,' Meg cried. 'We don't give up.'

Garth glanced at her briefly. He needed all his concentration for driving, but he saw her determined face, her eyes bright with unshed tears but her courage visible in the jut of her jaw and her clenched fists. His love for her was never stronger than at that moment. She was a tigress defending her young.

'We never give up,' he agreed, and was rewarded with a tight smile.

They drove over the shallow summit and over the other side, and there was the green sports car. Garth kept two cars between them, hoping Phillip wouldn't see their pursuit. After a few miles both cars turned off and they were directly behind him. The Maserati put on a burst of speed.

'He's clocked us,' Garth said.

They were already doing the maximum speed limit. Garth couldn't do any more. Since his car accident he'd had to gradually acclimatise to driving again. Now he was able to drive without flashbacks, but he wouldn't risk Meg or any of the other road users by driving far too fast.

'We're going to lose him,' Meg said in dismay as the green car sped away to a tiny coloured dot.

'I don't think so.'

The coloured dot grew larger and Garth saw why. Phillip was stuck in a long row of cars all caught behind a slow-moving red tractor. Now Garth and Meg were almost touching their bonnet to Phillip's boot. Meg strained against her seatbelt, searching for Katie. 'She's there, my darling's there.' And Garth heard the overwhelming relief in Meg's voice. He saw it too: the rim of a child's car seat in the back of the Maserati and the blonde curls above it. Katie's curls.

'What now?' Meg asked anxiously. 'We're hardly moving at all. I could almost get out and try to get into Phillip's car.'

'No, that's too dangerous,' Garth said, thinking fast. Could he corral Phillip's car somehow?

Before they could do anything, the green sports car suddenly whipped out of the slow-moving traffic jam and vanished left. Garth instinctively turned the steering wheel and followed. There was a well-hidden single-track road, tucked behind overgrown branches of blackthorn that went straight out away from the coastal road and into the bleak moors.

'He's going too fast. What is he thinking? If he crashes he could kill Katie,' Meg cried.

'That's not going to happen,' Garth replied with more confidence than he felt.

In reality, Phillip was going to get away. There was no way Garth's old car could catch up with the other man's brand-new expensive vehicle. Although he didn't voice it to Meg, he was determined that the police would get involved. Phillip wasn't going to get away with this. Partly, Garth blamed himself. He should've taken Meg's fears more seriously. He should've been there to protect her and Katie.

The green car was disappearing once more. Garth's car engine was making strange noises as it was pushed to extremes. A column of white steam burst from the bonnet and he started losing power. He floored the accelerator and got nothing. They were still moving forward on momentum and stored energy. Then a miracle took place. The sports car came to an abrupt halt ahead of them.

'Look!' Meg yelled. 'There's sheep on the road. He's completely stuck. We can get him, Garth. We can get Katie.'

Before Garth had even stopped the car, she was out and running like the wind, her hair streaming wildly. He glided to a halt in the empty moorland road. The green Maserati had slung sideways to avoid impact with the flock of sheep. As he got out of his car, Garth saw the door of the sports car fling open and Phillip's tall figure dash from it across the tarmac and onto the rough heather. Meg had dived into the car and Garth saw through the back window the two heads, dark and light, as mother and child were reunited.

Garth took off after the fleeing figure. The ground was rough and uneven and he cursed his shoes, which he'd chosen for the dance, not for pursuing fugitives on the moor. Before long, his chest was hurting from running fast and his breath came in gulps. Phillip was suffering too.

He'd slowed to a staggering lope, which still took him away across the tussocks and away from the road into a vast expanse of nowhere. Garth went on. He meant to tackle the other man and bring him down. He'd played rugby in his younger days, which would now be put to good use. His muscles began to warm up and his breathing eased. He found the rhythm of his run and almost began to enjoy it. He was gaining on his target. He was going to get him.

There was a cry and Phillip disappeared into the earth. Garth ran forwards in puzzlement. Was it a trick? Would Phillip loom up again? He barely avoided sliding into the quarry, teetering dangerously on the edge. The reddish soil crumbled under the soles of his feet and trickled down the steep slope to the bottom. There were dark pools of water down there and the earth looked treacherously muddy. He looked for Phillip. He'd rolled down the slope and now, covered in red mud, he was scrambling away up the far side where a stony outcrop provided some hand-holds.

There was a sharp pain in Garth's side — an excruciating stitch which made him gasp. He bent and touched his toes to try to stop it. When he stood up, it had eased. He looked across the quarry to see Phillip had made it up the other side. As he watched, the other man raised his arm in mock salute, then turned and jogged away.

When he got back to the cars, he saw Meg and Katie entwined in a long hug. Wearily, he went to them and all three huddled gratefully together.

'Where's Poppy's mummy?' Katie was asking. 'Daddy said I could talk to her. Poppy was sad with no mummy.'

'I don't know where Poppy's mummy is, Katie kid,' Meg told her gently. 'Why didn't you stay with Ben like you promised?'

Katie wiped her nose on her T-shirt but Meg didn't tell her off. 'I did stay with Ben,' she said indignantly, 'but Ben's mummy came to say hello to him. Then

211

I threw Poppy's ball and she ran after it. I went with Poppy. Then Daddy said I could see Poppy's mummy. That was okay, wasn't it?'

Meg kissed her. 'That was okay. But I don't want you running off again.'

'I want to go home now,' Katie said. 'Can we go to Garth's house? I want to paint.'

Meg took the car seat from Phillip's car and put it into Garth's. She settled Katie into it and came to speak quietly with Garth. 'Where did he go?'

Garth described his chase and Phillip's escape. 'When we leave, I'm sure he'll circle round and get back to his car. We need to call the police.'

'And I told you that I don't want to do that,' Meg replied sharply.

'He's still out there,' he said. 'He'll be a threat to you and Katie unless he's captured. Is that what you want?' Garth knew he was being too rough on her. She'd been through a lot that day, but he didn't like the idea that Phillip could come back. Couldn't she see that?

'He wouldn't hurt Katie,' Meg protested. 'He's misguided but he's not dangerous. He told Leila he wanted to be a father and he's gone about it all the wrong way, but that doesn't mean I should have him put in jail.'

Garth was suddenly angry with her. She'd got him involved with this. He'd driven like a madman over the coast and back country, chasing her ex-husband and finding her daughter. Didn't that count for something? Now she was blocking him out. The gulf between them was widening and he couldn't stop it.

'Why are you defending him now? The man's insane. He was stalking you and he kidnapped Katie.'

Meg looked away from him then turned back, shaking her head. 'I can't explain it to you. I know Phillip was keeping tabs on me and I didn't like it one bit. I was scared, yes, but deep down I didn't ever think he'd do more than intimidate me. He never physically hurt me. Why would he start now? It's always been cerebral with him. As for taking Katie, I know he'd never hurt her. He wanted to be a father. He just went about it all the wrong way.'

Garth gave an exasperated sigh. It was why he loved her, after all: her ability to empathise with others and to care deeply about them. But he didn't like it when her sympathy extended to her ex-husband. So what did that say about him? That he was all-out jealous of Phillip? It hurt that she excluded him from her decisions regarding both Phillip and Katie. If she truly was in love with him, wouldn't they share every decision, the large ones and the minute ones, together? She hadn't even trusted him enough to tell him she'd seen Phillip at the green.

Garth was bone-tired from the car chase. His anger fizzled into a smaller, much more melancholic mood. He was losing Meg before his very eyes, and before she was ever truly his. That was how it felt. She appeared oblivious to it and that made it a million times worse.

She was sitting in the car now, waiting for him to drive them all back to Burley. Garth got into the driver's seat slowly. Katie had fallen asleep in the back, worn out from all the excitement of the day.

'Are you all right?' Meg asked him.

*Are we all right?* That was the question. And Garth didn't want to think about the answer to that. The air had shifted, changed between them. He was no longer sure about anything. 'Yes, I'm fine. A little tired. That's all. What about you?' He was aware he sounded formally polite and tried to ignore her surprised expression.

'I'm just happy to get Katie back. I want to go home now to the cottage and sleep for a hundred years.' Meg's tone was deliberately light and joking. He was meant to smile and share her joke.

But he couldn't. Home to the cottage, she'd said. Not Winter Farm. It was like a message for Garth. She didn't consider his house to be her home. And if that was the case, what did she really, truly feel about him? It is said that home is where the heart is. So where did Meg's heart really lie?

# 13

All her dreams had turned to dust. Meg knelt on the kitchen floor, her hair pushed back from her face with a flowered scarf and a scrubbing brush in her hand. A pail of warm, soapy water was placed on the tiles, the water already grey with use. However much she scrubbed and cleaned and polished the cottage, she couldn't avoid her memories. She relived the terrible moment when Katie went missing and the sight of Ben's distraught face. She thundered along endless roads in Garth's car, searching and searching for Phillip.

She got up and peeled off her yellow rubber gloves. Had she locked the front door? She went to it and checked the locks. She gave the doorknob a good rattle and felt the solidness of it. It wouldn't yield. Next she tiptoed upstairs and pushed the door to Katie's bedroom open just a tiny sliver. Her daughter breathed heavily and regularly, one arm flung up on the pillow, the other curved tightly round Belly Bear.

Coming back down the steps, she saw the telephone where she'd left it in plain view on top of the spindly stool in the hall. It no longer rang in the middle of the night. She was glad of that. She no longer felt as if Phillip was watching her either. He hadn't made contact since the day of his escape across the moors. She felt his absence and should've been at peace. Instead there was a restlessness to her that refused to dampen down.

Primrose Cottage no longer felt safe. It was full of painful memories and hadn't turned out to be the sanctuary she'd hoped for. She and Katie were voluntary prisoners there with the doors locked against the outside. And Garth. She didn't know what to think. He was angry with her, she sensed that. She tried to explain to him why she didn't want the police involved, but she hadn't made much headway. She knew he felt shut out, but she didn't understand how to change that. She loved him so much, and he loved her, and yet it wasn't working. That was the most painful acknowledgement of all. It was as if there was a vast chasm and she couldn't make the jump to reach him.

There was no more talk of her moving to Winter Farm. It had been a couple of weeks since the barbecue and they'd hardly spoken to each other except to agree not to tell anyone the dramatic events of the day. To Tabby, Meg had merely said she'd been tired and Garth had taken her and Katie home early. Tabby had scrutinised her but didn't argue. Ben had been too busy talking to his mother to tell anyone about what had happened, and Garth had phoned him as soon as Katie was safe and asked him to keep quiet about it all.

Meg went back to wiping the kitchen cupboards down. After that she planned to start on the living room, vacuuming and polishing and washing the skirting boards. By then Katie would be awake and she'd make some lunch. The everyday, humdrum routines of family life. A barrier against her nightmares, and yet not sufficient in this place. She was acutely conscious of the wide landscape beyond the cottage walls where someone could watch them with binoculars from any vantage point. She missed London now. There was safety in numbers. There she could melt into the crowded streets. It didn't need to be Tottenham. There were other areas where she could possibly afford a house or apartment.

Her head ached from the conclusions she was gradually reaching. When the doorbell rang she dropped the sponge, and soap suds splattered over her jeans, soaking them in dark patches. Cautiously, she moved to the door. There was a chain now, so she opened it but kept the chain hooked.

'It's me. Can I come in?' Ben asked.

She took off the chain and let him in.

Poppy was at his heels as usual. The puppy was growing rapidly, almost fitting its large paws, but not quite.

'How are you?' Ben said, standing tall and awkwardly in her hallway.

She gestured him in to the living room, Poppy pushing at her legs to follow him. 'Did Garth send you to say that?' Meg asked sadly.

He looked surprised. 'No. I was just asking, that's all. Anyway, I came to tell you I'm leaving. I'm going home.'

'Oh Ben, that's great news. I'm so happy for you.' Meg sat down opposite him. Poppy thumped her tail and stared up at Meg from Ben's side with soft brown eyes.

'Yeah, well, Mum asked me to give them a chance, so I sort of had to, you know. He's not so bad as step-fathers go, and my step-sister was never the problem. I'll go back for a while and see.'

'You're doing the right thing,' Meg said, smiling at him. 'Your mother must be delighted.'

'Yeah.' He nodded, then hesitated. 'Thing is, I've got a favour to ask you. It's Poppy. Where my mum lives, well it's a tiny terraced house and there's no room for a dog. I thought . . . well, Katie loves Poppy.' His voice was choked up and he coughed and rubbed his face furiously.

Meg pretended not to see the shininess in his eyes. 'Of course we'll look after Poppy for you. It's a shame you can't take her with you, but she's welcome here.'

Ben didn't speak. He stroked the puppy's head and she gave a little bark and wagged her tail. He stood up and gave Meg the handle of the lead. She secured it under the leg of the sofa and shut the living room door as they went out. They both heard Poppy whine.

Ben turned to Meg as they reached the gate. 'Is there something wrong between you and Garth? He's unhappy and it's not just because I'm leaving. Can't you sort it out?'

Ben was eighteen, but it was the boy

in him that was asking. The world was still a place of black and white, and the shades and shadows yet to be experienced. Meg shook her head.

'I don't know what's wrong. It's not Garth's fault, it's mine, but I can't fix it somehow.'

'He loves you very much,' Ben said. 'He doesn't come straight out and say it — that would be mushy, but I can tell he does.'

'Goodbye, Ben. Will you write and let me know how you're getting on?' Meg said, the sadness pulling her down like waterweeds in a deep pool.

'Yes, I'll write you. Bye.'

★   ★   ★

The sound of mournful howling filled the cottage. Meg felt like joining the dog, raising her throat to the full moon and letting all her sorrow rip out of her. Katie cuddled Poppy and tried to soothe her with nursery rhymes and snatches of song. Driven almost to despair, Meg finally phoned Tabby for help.

Before long, Tabby had arrived and insisted on taking both child and dog with her on the family trip to a nearby beach. At least there the noise of the hound would be lost to the sea air and the distraction of five children might help a little. Would Meg like to join them? Meg declined. She had a monster headache and thought to lie down for an hour. With promises to bring back a much calmer puppy, Tabby's car drew away with a friendly toot of the horn. Meg went upstairs to lie down.

The phone rang. She struggled up out of a thick, syrupy sleep and hurried downstairs to answer it. She half expected an empty line with nothing but sinister air at the other end. But it was Garth. He hadn't popped round as he had done previously, but had telephoned instead. Did he think there was no welcome for him here? Meg thought miserably.

'How are you?' he asked, echoing Ben's words. She couldn't guess his emotions over the line.

'Fine, and you?' she asked politely.

A tinny rush of electric air, then his voice again. 'We need to talk. Shall I come over?'

'I'll come to you,' she replied hastily.

She wanted out of the cottage. Away from the locks on the doors and the smell of frightened dog and the overwhelming essence of disappointment pervading the house; she'd failed to make the new life she wanted here. Phillip had spoiled it irrevocably. Wherever he was, he had won.

The air was distinctly autumnal as she walked the familiar slope up to Winter Farm. There was a chill to the day and the smell of old earth as the summer crumbled. Here and there toadstools sprouted in amongst the grasses, releasing a ripe odour as her feet brushed them. Around the farmhouse the rowans were in full crimson berry, laden with a good harvest from the weeks of sunshine. Rain was forecast for the afternoon and the rest of the week.

Garth was waiting for her on the front porch. His tall broad-shouldered frame filled it. His expression was unreadable and Meg felt awkward and stiff, like a stranger to him. Had they ever kissed passionately? Had he ever reached for her in desire and love in this very house? It was as if it had happened to someone else and in a different time.

'Can I get you a drink?' Garth asked, as if she was any guest arriving at his house.

'No, thank you.' She could be just as polite and give nothing away.

'Meg . . . ' He looked as if he'd move towards her and she stilled in anticipation, but he didn't. He turned away and moved to the conservatory at the back of the house, expecting her to follow. She did so, thinking that this could've been her house too. It was a lovely home, tastefully decorated and understated. She wondered if Anna had chosen the blue colours on the walls and tiles, the terracotta and Spanish curlicues on the conservatory walls.

'Ben came to see me,' Meg said, for want of a way to start the conversation and choosing a topic they could agree on. 'He says he's going home. You'll miss him.'

'I will miss him,' Garth agreed. 'I got used to the sound of someone else in the house.' He looked at her with his dark blue eyes and she nearly ran to him. How easy it would be to curl up against his broad chest and shut out the world. How neatly it would all slot into place if she suggested he needn't lose the sound of others in the house.

But it was all too complicated. Phillip was out there somewhere. She didn't know what he'd do next, if anything. If she and Katie moved to Winter Farm, were they going to be any safer? It was still out in the countryside, approachable from all angles. Garth might be at risk too. But it wasn't just that. She trusted Garth, but he didn't believe she did. Saying it didn't seem to convince him. There was a broken piece to their love and she didn't know how to fix it.

'He's left Poppy with us,' Meg went on, the sound of her own voice falsely bright, irritating her.

'Yes, he said he was going to do that. If you don't want the dog, Alex will take it for you.'

'No, it's fine. Katie loves her. Anyway, I'm hoping Ben might be able to take her back at some point. However small a house, there's surely room for a puppy. He might be able to persuade his mother to take Poppy in.'

'What about us?' Garth asked quietly.

There it was. The question she was trying to avoid. Her headache came back, pulsing strongly on the bone of her temple.

'I love you,' he said.

'I love you too.' Meg's voice cracked on the words. 'But it's not that simple.'

'Then we make it simple. What's to be said? I'm sorry we argued about Phillip and the way to deal with him. There.'

She was faintly irritated by the puff of air that came out with the 'there'.

Did he still blame her for not trusting him?

'I don't feel safe here anymore,' she said, trying to explain.

'Then let me help you feel safe,' Garth said. 'Move in with me and I'll look after both of you.'

Meg shook her head and backed away. 'It won't work. I need a bit of space to think about all this. I have to get away from the cottage and from Devon. It was a mistake thinking I could start all over again afresh. I'm going back to London for a while.'

There was a stunned silence from Garth. She hadn't meant to blurt it out, but there it was. Her thinking was done. In her mind, she meant only that she required a break.

How long, she wasn't sure. It could be days or possibly weeks. But she was coming back. He misunderstood her and his retort was savage with barely hidden pain.

'Don't let me stop you then. If that's what you want, then go. Go!'

'Garth . . . '

'Go, Meg. It's over, whatever it was we thought we had.' He was shaking his head, his lips tight and the skin around them white.

Through her tears she watched him open the door and wait for her to leave. She opened her mouth to try to explain but he wouldn't connect with her. She moved quickly past him. He didn't want her there. He was right. It was over. The love she thought she'd found to last a lifetime, the love she thought this time she'd got right, had gone horribly wrong. Now all she wanted to do was flee.

She ran back down the hill, half slipping on the mud as the forecast rain thudded in large drops into the parched ground. The sky was dark with it and the cottage looked dull and humped under the grey clouds. She let herself in and slammed the door. A sob burst from her throat and she gave way to her despair and let the tears stream out until she was raw and empty.

When she was hollow, Meg washed her face and made a pot of tea. Her movements were leaden and she almost didn't feel anything besides numbness. She sat at the kitchen table and replayed what had happened. If Garth loved her and she loved him, then why, why couldn't it work? Talking had made it worse. Whatever she said, he misconstrued, and vice-versa. Now he thought she meant to leave Primrose Cottage forever and move back to London, which was not her intention at all. Why couldn't he understand her need for breathing space? He wanted her to run straight to him. But he didn't understand her fear of the openness around the farm. If she was afraid of Phillip returning, then he'd only urge her to contact the police. The argument went round and round in circles.

Meg began to feel that if they couldn't agree on this important issue, then did they have the basis for a good marriage in any case? Communication and trust were such vital ingredients to any relationship, and yet she and Garth were failing with both. Her throat tightened and she swallowed convulsively. No, there were to be no more tears. She'd cried enough. She had to accept it was over between them. The hollowness took hold of her; along with a sadness so deep she could see no end to it.

She was back where she'd always been. There was just her and Katie. And Katie's welfare and happiness came first. Katie had loved London, their tiny flat and Kanga, the next-door cat. Didn't it make sense to go back? They could hide there. Phillip might not expect that, if he was even still in the country. She thought of Leila flying out to her retreat in the Bahamas, so certain that her husband didn't know of it. Yet Phillip knew everyone's secrets. He winkled them out with the aid of his private investigator. He could be out there in the Bahamas even now, tracking his second wife. Not that Meg wished that on Leila by any means.

She put down her mug and went into the hall. The telephone was there. She took a deep sigh and picked up the receiver. She'd make the call, then drive over to the beach where Katie was enjoying an afternoon of fun with Tabby's family. Tabby wouldn't be pleased with Meg's decision, but that couldn't be helped. She knew now she was doing the right thing.

'Hello. Is that Anstruther's Estate Agency? Yes, I'd like to put my cottage on the market please.'

\* \* \*

Garth was in anguish. He had messed up thoroughly. When he invited Meg over he wanted to get everything out in the open and talk freely about his feelings and hers, so they could put it all behind them and plan their future together. *Together*. She was all he wanted. So why was it so difficult for them to find harmony? He loved her with a passion and intensity that shocked him.

But she was blocking him out. She was running back to London and leaving him. Shouldn't that tell him that she didn't love him back? She might say she was in love with him, but it wasn't enough to stop her going. He had to accept that. With a cry of mingled pain and rage, Garth flung his paintbrush down. In his agitation after Meg left, he'd tried to paint, to absorb himself. But it wasn't working. All he could see was her face: those large grey eyes which he no longer could read. What did she want? Clearly not him. He wasn't enough for her; otherwise she and Katie would be living here at Winter Farm. He had been going to propose to her today. Garth took out the box which held his grandmother's ring and put it on top of the bookcase. If she didn't like it, then he had planned to invite her to shop for another one with him.

He pushed back the easel. The canvas, wet with the first brushstrokes, slid askew but he didn't right it. He was a fool. What did it matter if they were out of sorts with each other? He needed to try again. He loved her so deeply. That was what was important. He would go down to the cottage and tell her that. Whatever misunderstandings there were, and whatever gap there was dividing them, none of it mattered. They could sort it all out given time.

He took the small jewellery box and slid it into his pocket. With more confident strides, he covered the ground from Winter Farm to Primrose Cottage quickly, ignoring the rain that soaked his shirt and dripped down the back of his neck.

He pushed the buzzer and heard it ring out inside Meg's home. It rang out and rang out and rang out. Meg was gone.

# 14

'I don't want to go!' Katie wailed. 'I want to stay with you.'

'But you like painting and playing in the sand pit,' Meg said desperately. 'What about the nice friends you've made? It'll be lovely to play with them today, won't it?'

'No.' Katie's small face was mutinous.

'Yes!' Meg felt like a small child too, playing verbal tit-for-tat to see who lasted longest and won.

'No!' Katie screamed and slapped Meg.

'That's enough, young lady. You're going to nursery and that's that!' Meg shouted. 'Now put your feet in your wellies and don't answer back.'

She managed to get the wellies onto two protesting, fat wriggly legs and buttoned Katie's coat up. The snow was falling thickly and lying on the pavements and roads as they walked the few minutes up the road to the nursery school, Meg holding Katie's mittened hand tightly. The traffic went past, spraying up brown slush. It was December and only two weeks until Christmas.

'I want Poppy,' Katie said miserably. 'Why can't we go home?'

'This is home now, darling,' Meg answered. 'You know we couldn't bring Poppy with us. It wouldn't be fair. She's much happier in the countryside.'

'Can we visit her?'

'I've explained this to you already. We can't visit for a while. Maybe when we've settled in a bit more we'll go back.'

'I miss Jane. She won't know I've started nursery school.'

'Well you told her on the phone, so she does know.'

Meg knew her answers were feeble. The truth of the matter was that Katie hadn't settled back in Tottenham as well as Meg had hoped. Neither of them had. Katie missed the cottage and the dog and Tabby's children. Meg missed Garth. The hollowness had become an ever-present ache. But pride wouldn't let her call him. He didn't want her enough, it was clear. He hadn't tried to make contact with her. It was over and she had to move on with her life. And she was trying. She really was. But it was so difficult. She was lucky her tenant had moved out suddenly and that she was able to live in her flat at all.

She waved and put on a cheerful face as Katie walked forlornly into the red brick building that served as the local nursery school. There were no grass or shrubs, just tarmac and a scruffy tree with blackened, slimy branches. Meg didn't know what kind of tree it was. But it looked sick, whatever it was — bowed down with broken limbs where kids had swung up on it and snapped them off. The nursery was crowded on three sides by terraced houses, some with boarded-up windows and others with tatty curtains and litter lacing their front yards. Here and there people had made an effort and there was fresh paint on the walls and sills and neat slabbed fronts. The fresh snow made it all seem a little grimy though.

She thought briefly of Devon. How nicely the snow would be lying on the fields and the thatch of the cottage. What it would be like having snow on the beach. Would it lie thickly on the round pebbles, and would it melt as it met the sea?

She let herself into the flat and sighed heavily. For some reason the wallpaper was peeling off the living room wall. There was no sign of a damp problem and the man she called out had metered it and shrugged, telling her there was no problem because it was dry. The real problem was that she had no money to re-decorate. Her plan to move to another part of London had fallen away. Until she sold the cottage they were going nowhere. The estate agent had been rather gloomy when she phoned him last.

'It's the credit crunch, Mrs Lyons, I'm afraid. Properties just aren't selling as quickly as they used to.'

'But a lovely cottage in such a delightful setting? Surely someone must want it?' Meg thought she could be an estate agent, the way she described her home. She could almost see Mr Anstruther shaking his head at the other end of the line.

'Unfortunately, even those who do want it are at the mercy of the economic situation. There's no chain, you see. They can't sell their houses and so they can't buy yours. Simple, but not very helpful in your situation. I'll be in touch if we have any interest in it. Good day.'

So they were stuck in the flat for the time being. A very tiny part of her was glad that Primrose Cottage hadn't sold immediately. It meant there was a link to Garth still and a glimmer of hope. She knew if he got in touch and told her he loved her that she'd go back in an instant. But it hadn't happened in three months, so she doubted it ever would. As the days and weeks went by it was more and more unlikely he'd change his mind. Despite his declaration of love for her, it seemed it wasn't enough for him to want her back.

Her mobile buzzed in her pocket and she took it out. There was a new text message. She clicked on it. It was from Ben. He'd kept in touch after he returned to the city and she'd met him once for lunch. She knew he had found a job so there weren't many spare hours, besides which he presumably had a bunch of friends to hang out with. She was glad he texted occasionally.

*Can I come over? In your area right now.*

She glanced reluctantly at her desk. There wasn't much room in the cramped living room, but she had pushed it up against the window to get the best of the light and squashed the sofa up as far as it would go on the opposite wall. There was just enough space to sit at the desk without other furniture pressing against her. The desk itself was piled high with paper and files which threatened to tumble onto her laptop. She had a lot of work to do. She spent far too long simply staring out the window at the street below. Not seeing it.

*Of course. I'll put coffee pot on.*

He arrived covered in a frosting of snowflakes which left a wet trail on her carpet. Ben shook off his beanie hat and jacket and looked about vaguely for a place to dump them. Meg retrieved them before they landed on the floor and hung them up on the brass peg behind the door.

'How are you?' she asked, smiling at him.

He shrugged and hunched his shoulders. He looked different — older and even thinner, if that was possible. The tip of his nose was pink with the cold. A fashionably shaped beard straggled on his lips and chin and he was wearing a navy work jacket with a red scribble logo. 'Paul's Pizzas', it read.

'Where's your bike?' Meg asked.

Ben delivered pizzas around a large area of north London. It didn't pay particularly well but it was a job, which was more than most of his mates had.

'I left it chained up to the lamp-post. It'll be fine.' He took the hot coffee gratefully and didn't speak again until he'd drained it.

'It's nice to see you,' Meg said, placing a plate of biscuits in front of him.

'But why am I here?' Ben finished her sentence for her, with a grin that had no mirth in it.

'Is everything okay?'

'No, not really,' he said with a heavy sigh. 'Not at all, in fact. I'm beginning to see that while my mum and my step-dad Brian wanted me home again, nothing's really changed. The house isn't big enough for all of us, the way things are going.'

'What do you mean? Are you going to move out?'

'I'm not sure. I haven't thought it through properly. Mum and Brian argue a lot about money. He lost his job and can't find another. Then there's Kitty, my little sister. She needs stuff for school, clothes and so on. It doesn't help that I'm there eating the food and taking up space. I sleep in the living room because there's no extra bedroom and I'm bringing home some wages but not enough.'

'Oh Ben. You can come here if you want. You still wouldn't have a bedroom, but it might help you and your family.' Meg wasn't sure how they'd manage if Ben took up her offer, but she couldn't bear the look of unhappiness on his face.

'I want to go back to Winter Farm,' he said. 'I hate delivering pizzas. I hate the busy roads and the way the cars don't care about cyclists. I've been knocked off my bike once and nearly knocked off . . . well, I can't count them.'

'Back to Winter Farm,' Meg echoed faintly.

'You wanted to help me, Meg. Well you can. You can contact Garth and ask him if I can come back and work on the farm with him and Alex. I can get Poppy back and train her up to be a working farm dog.' Ben's voice was suddenly eager.

'I can't do that. I'm sorry, Ben. I . . . I've lost contact with Garth.'

'Can't, or won't?' Ben's voice rose in annoyance at her. 'What happened with you and Garth? I thought you loved each other. He certainly loved you. How did you spoil it?'

'I don't want to talk about it, please,' Meg said. 'Look, I can't phone Garth, but I can give you some money to tide you over until you decide where you're going.'

Not that she could afford to give her money away, but she felt a responsibility towards the young man. She cared what happened to him. But she couldn't make that first move towards Garth, not even for Ben. How could she face his rejection if she tried to speak to him? If he wanted her back then he'd have been in touch by now.

'I don't want your money,' Ben said in dismay. 'I want to change my life. ˙ want to go back to Devon. But only

Garth really wants me there. I thought
. . . I hoped you'd pave the way for me,
yeah. Suss him out, you know.'

'I just can't. That part of my life is
finished.'

*Can't, or won't?* Ben's angry question haunted her after he'd gone. She
walked back along to the nursery to
pick Katie up early. The snow had
stopped but it lay in drifts and topped
the trees and surfaces, reminding her
that Christmas was so nearly upon
them. What would the holiday season
bring? She wanted to make it a happy
festival for Katie. If Ben was still in
London she could invite him over.
*Can't, or won't?* Was she being stupidly
proud and stubborn? It would be so
easy to ring Garth's phone number; but
if he answered, what would she say? She
didn't know if he'd even care anymore
whether she phoned or not. On her last
call to Tabby, her friend had told her
she hadn't seen him in the village in a
while. She imagined him holed up at
Winter Farm reclusively once more.

The nursery smelt of institutional warmed food, chalk and poster paints, and stale gym socks. The noise of children's chatter echoed through the high-ceilinged rooms, and somewhere a class was singing about a happy hippo and its many friends. She stood on tiptoe and looked through the glass circle into Katie's classroom before entering. Her daughter was tipping sand out of a green bucket into a plastic flowerpot. She looked contented. When Meg went in, Katie didn't want to go home. She was having fun. Meg felt tired and drained. No matter what she did, she wasn't pleasing anyone.

They went outside into the bitingly cold air. Meg stooped to button up Katie's coat. A dark figure loomed over her as she stood up.

'Hello, Meg.'

'Look Mummy, it's Daddy. He knows Poppy's mummy.'

It was Phillip. Instinctively she clutched Katie to her. She looked about. There was no one going in or ou of the nursery school. There were pedestrians along the narrow street, but they were all huddled against the freezing weather and no one made eye contact.

'You needn't worry; I'm hardly likely to grab your child in broad daylight,' Phillip said with a hint of mockery.

'You've got a cheek turning up here,' Meg snapped. 'I should call the police.'

'But you won't,' was his rejoinder. 'And you didn't before, for which I thank you,' he acknowledged with a bend of his head. 'Can we talk somewhere out of this icy breeze?'

She hesitated.

'Please, Meg. It won't take long.'

Bemused by his almost humble tone, she nodded. They ended up in a cafe a couple of streets away. It had smeared windows and a faded green sign, but it was warm inside and the waitress was friendly. The coffee when it arrived was surprisingly good, and Katie was soon absorbed in her slice of cake and a glass of juice with a colourful straw.

'I came to apologise. I put you through a lot of pain,' Phillip said.

She was taken aback. It was the last thing she imagined him saying. Was it some kind of trick he was playing?

'You look suspicious, but you don't need to be,' Phillip went on. 'I want you to know that I'm letting you go. I don't need you anymore.'

How typical of him. He still had to be in control and it was all about him, not her.

'You're letting me go. I should thank you then,' Meg said with barely hidden sarcasm.

'You're angry with me. I can see that. But yes, you should thank me. You can get on with your life now.'

'And Katie?' Meg spoke in a low voice so that Katie wouldn't pay attention. The little girl was singing and drawing pictures now on the steamy window.

'That was a mistake, I grant you. I had an idea in my head of being a father. Of having an heir to leave my wealth to. But it isn't your child, Meg. It's all changed now.'

She didn't understand all of what he was saying. He was so self-absorbed it was as if she was meant to simply know what he was on about. It was enough to know he wasn't going to try and take Katie away from her again.

'I am aware that I have issues. It was wrong of me to try to take Katie. I can see that now. I do appreciate you keeping the authorities out of it. It won't happen again.' He toyed with the coffee cup but didn't drink any. Meg's own cup was untouched and the liquid gone cold. She couldn't relax in his company. She needed to hear what he had to say, then she wanted him gone.

'Are you getting help?' she asked.

'I went to the Bahamas to see Leila,' Phillip said conversationally, and she wondered whether he'd heard her question. 'She was very surprised to see me. She had no idea I knew about her little hideaway home there.' He chuck-led.

Meg shivered and wrapped her cardigan more firmly round her. 'What did you do to her?'

Phillip raised an eyebrow. 'Do? Nothing at all. I have no further interest in her. But while I was there, I met a friend of hers. An amazing woman who I can talk to and who listens to me. I realise I never truly loved either you or Leila. But that I am also to blame for a lot of the errors in the marriages. I am getting help. I'm learning about myself and how I function. It's fascinating.'

Meg doubted that Phillip would ever be anything but completely selfish, but at least it sounded as if he was beginning to realise his own faults.

'I came to say goodbye, Meg. I'm moving to the United States to start afresh. I'm moving my businesses over there, so it's a completely new life for me. I wanted you to know that. If you ever wish to visit, here's my card.'

Reluctantly she took the business card and made a show of putting it in her handbag. She would never use it.

'I wish you luck in your future,' Phillip said, standing and putting on his expensive wool coat and scarf. 'I hope it works out with your new partner. Goodbye, Katie.'

Katie waved and went back to eating cake, uninterested in him.

The flat was cold when they got in and Meg hurried to turn on the central heating. 'Shall we have a TV dinner?' she asked Katie. It was a small treat to offer, but she suddenly looked forward to snuggling up with her daughter on the sofa, watching television and sharing toasted cheese sandwiches.

As she turned on the grill and got the cheese grater and the block of cheddar from her fridge, Meg thought about what Ben had said. She could help him. She could get in touch with Garth if she chose to do so. If she was prepared for disappointment. She thought about Phillip leaving. It changed things. He was no longer a dark shadow on the edges of her consciousness. She was finally free from him.

A shot of hope, like a ray of morning sunlight, burst through her. She could make that effort and be the first one to get in touch. She'd tell him how she felt. How she missed him so badly it made her ache. She would tell him why she'd run away back to London and why she was finally ready to return. She and Katie could move back into Primrose Cottage and she and Garth could take time to get to know each other all over again.

With a flush of excited happiness she took the meal through to the living room. She fetched a blanket for Katie and turned the television on. While Katie ate, she'd make that call. There was no reason to wait. She put the tray of sandwiches down beside the little girl and went to the phone.

It rang before she could use it. She picked up the receiver and listened. 'It's Anstruther's Estate Agency here with rather a good piece of news for you. We've managed to sell your cottage.'

# 15

'Wow, you've been busy.' Gilda Mable was counting up the number of paintings stacked ready to go to the London gallery. 'I like the theme — very nice; very atmospheric with the charcoals, the greys, the shades of blue. Lovely. They'll sell well.'

Garth didn't care if they sold well or not. The paintings had poured out of him from his very soul and he had to express his feelings somehow. If the results made Gilda pleased and earned him money, well that was a side effect. He got little enjoyment from his art these days but it kept him busy, along with the running of the farm. Alex hadn't let him escape from his duties once he'd shown some interest in them while Ben was there.

'So these are ready to go, yes?' Gilda asked. She was unusually hesitant and

Garth knew she wanted something. She stood and twisted her rings on her fingers. Gilda loved jewellery and had a ring on every finger. Gold and silver and a long turquoise inset stone graced her mobile hands. She wore a long, thick cotton skirt and a man's shirt and waistcoat over it. Her grey hair flowed down almost to her waist and was kept back with a girlish Alice band. But nobody who knew her was fooled by her eclectic fashion sense. Gilda was as sharp as tacks when it came to art and the business of investing in it and selling it. She was one of the cleverest people Garth knew.

'It's the gallery,' she said. 'They want to hold a special exhibition of your work and they want to invite you to be there for the drinks reception.'

'No,' Garth replied abruptly. 'You know the deal. I paint the pictures and you sell them for me. The gallery takes its cut and we all get richer. I don't show up in person, ever.'

'Yes, yes,' she said quickly. 'But I

thought, perhaps . . . this had changed. Over the summer your paintings were lighter in mood and you yourself, too. Not this theme though.' Gilda put down her net book and stared at him hard. 'As your agent I have to advise you to attend this party at the gallery. It will be good for business.'

He wanted to throw the idea out immediately, but the fact was that there were various projects on the farm that needed doing. Alex had a list of them. Without more funds, Garth couldn't tell his farm manager to go ahead.

'When is the drinks reception?' he asked.

Gilda clapped her hands in triumph. 'You will go? Excellent. The party is next Saturday in the centre of London. I'll be in touch with the details.'

'I didn't agree to go.'

'We both know you will, so I'll send the email to you and you do as it directs, yes? I'll be there, too, and we can sell many of your lovely paintings that night, I am confident of it.'

256

When she had gone, Garth put on his boots and coat and went outside into the frosty air. He intended to walk to Anna's Field and let the snowy landscape blast some energy into him. He wasn't sleeping well and hadn't for months. Not since Meg left. He tramped down the hill to take the lane past the cottage and go through the gate. His feet crimped the snow with a muted sound and a few stray snowflakes caressed his cheek, warning of more to come. It was cold enough for more snow.

So he was going up to London. He couldn't help thinking of Meg. She lived there, but it was so huge that obviously they wouldn't meet by chance. He'd come to the conclusion that she was better off without him. He'd rushed to the cottage that day on impulse with the ring, but she was out. Maybe that had been for the best. He'd had the rest of the day to mull it all over. She was leaving him and Devon to return to her old life in the city. After all, she was city girl at heart. Had she ever really intended to stay in the countryside, or was it a brief whim? There had been something special that had grown between them, but had withered on the stem in the end. He could blame himself or Meg or Phillip and the dramatic events surrounding them. But in the end, he was doing them both a favour by not pursuing her further.

What did he have to offer her? He was a farmer in a rural area — very different from the cityscape she loved. He would never leave this land. Then there was Anna. People had long memories. Although they had accepted him in the village the day of the barbecue, there would always be rumours and suspicion about him. It wasn't fair to draw Meg into that. No, she was better off without him. If only he could forget her.

He was outside the cottage now. Vinny's cottage, as he always thought of it. Primrose Cottage to Meg and Katie. The 'for sale' sign had been taken down. The cottage was empty, the windows blank and uninviting, and the thatch black with melted snow. He had bought it on impulse. It seemed the right thing to do somehow. He couldn't bear the idea of other people living there when his memories were full of Meg and Katie bringing it to life. He told himself he didn't want new neighbours so close to Winter Farm. Apart from Alex and occasional visits from Gilda, he wasn't seeing anyone these days. It suited him. He could paint in peace. Occasional creaks and friendly groans from the old farm's timbers reminded him of the summer days when Ben was living there. He pushed aside any regrets on that front. Ben had his own life to lead back with his family. He tried not to think of Meg visiting and of the day it had turned to passion and love for both of them upstairs.

Anna's Field was stark with rows and furrows of dark earth and white snow. The trees were all bare limbs pointing to the metal sky, and a flock of crows were hunched on them like waitir shadows. Garth's breath was white mist and he shoved his hands into his pockets to warm them.

'Garth!' It was Alex Cranborn, arm raised in greeting and coming down from the top of the field towards him.

Garth smiled. Finally he had got Alex to use his first name. He waited for the older man to catch up.

'The barrels of feed have arrived. I'm wanting to put 'em in the near barn. Not much room, like.'

'Are you saying you won't get them all in?' Alex had a habit of making quiet statements which Garth had to interpret.

'It's the car. Under the tarpaulin. Takes up space.' Alex sounded gruffly uncomfortable.

Later he forced himself to go up to the barn. He stood there and listened to the silence. There was a sharp tang like yeast from the barrels. Alex was right. The bulky tarpaulin took up far too much room. It was a waste of his barn. Garth took hold of the edge of the tarp and pulled. It slithered off and lay in a crumpled pool at his feet. There was a stain of old oil under the car. He saw anew the crushed bonnet and mashed metal and brittle glass of the aftermath of the accident. He waited for the pain and the guilt to torture him. This was his atonement to Anna. But this time there was nothing but a bittersweet regret for all that had occurred and all that had not.

'Goodbye, Anna,' he whispered softly. 'I hope you've forgiven me for not loving you enough. Because finally, I've forgiven myself for the past.'

The tractor was a powerful machine. The heavy chain and giant iron hook were attached to the car fender, and Garth started up the tractor engine. With a whine and a metallic crunch it began to drag the car like a wounded beast out of the wide barn doors. He dumped it as far down the fields as possible to the access road. In the morning he'd ask Alex to arrange for it to be taken to the dump.

* * *

'I don't usually write articles about art,' Meg said down the phone. 'It's not a subject I'm very knowledgeable about.'

'If I was you I wouldn't mention that to the editor,' the girl at the other end said snidely. 'Look, do you want it or not? If not, I have other writers who'll jump at the chance to go to a snazzy party and drink free wine.'

Meg doubted there were many who'd be willing to give up their Saturday evening at such short notice. It wasn't a big magazine with a large circulation, just a community mag which paid hardly anything, but the girl was right. She wasn't in a position to choose. The wallpaper was still peeling off the walls and getting worse. The radiator in the bathroom didn't work, except to gurgle annoyingly, and a shelf in the kitchen had spontaneously fallen off one of its brackets that day. The money from the sale of the cottage would help enormously, but it hadn't come in yet.

'There's some artist bod coming along to promote his work,' the girl went on. 'Can you get a quote from him and a few piccies? I'll email you the address of the gallery in a mo.'

'I'll have to organise a baby-sitter.' Meg spoke her gathering thoughts out loud.

There was a snort on the other end of the line. 'Not my problem. If you can't do this, tell me now.'

'No, I can do it. I'll get the copy to you early tomorrow,' she promised quickly.

She rang off with more promises of a prompt response and good photographs. Once the funds from the sale of Primrose Cottage came through, she'd have breathing space to decide what she wanted to do. She should be glad it had sold, but it made her sad. Her last tie to Devon and to Garth had gone. While she owned the cottage there was always a slim but fastened bond to him and to the place. Now it was no more. The worst thing was discovering that he wa the new owner. He had bought her out to get rid of her. He didn't want her coming back. It hurt her dreadfully, but she tried to ignore it and to forget him. So far that hadn't worked. She thought about him every day.

Meg's neighbour was only too glad to come and baby-sit for Katie. She loved the company of the little girl and missed her own kids, grown up and away as they were and hardly visiting. Meg wasn't sure what to wear. She was going to the art gallery to work, but she'd have to mingle with the guests, so her scruffy jeans and old cardigan wouldn't do. She laid various outfits on the bed and tried them on. In the end she settled for a peach-coloured jersey dress and matched it with a pair of nude high heels. She fastened a chunky coral bead necklace around her neck and made her face up with a light touching of powder, lipstick and eye shadow. Unsure about her hair, she left it loose to curl on her shoulders. She grabbed her coat and bag and checked she had her small tape recorder and camera.

She took the Tube into central London. It was jammed with crowds of people going out for their Saturday-night entertainment. She'd forgotten how sociable it could be. Her usual Saturday night was staying in with Katie, playing board games or drawing with crayons. When Katie was in bed, she had a solitary late dinner and ended up reading a book by lamplight without any music or television which might disturb her daughter's slumber. Although she was going to the gallery to work, it was like a night out. She smiled. *Way to go, Meg. A whole evening out with your camera and recorder, and then home to write up an article in the wee small hours for the deadline.* A woman sitting opposite her in the tube looked at her suspiciously. People who smiled and muttered to themselves were to be avoided.

The underground station flowed like a river in both directions as people left and entered, shoving past each other a gaily coloured stream. Meg took out the printed-off map with the address and directions of the gallery. It wasn't far away — an easy walk even in her high heels. She saw the place when she turned into the street. Its lights were bright and there were fairy lights, too, lining the windows. Laughter and chatter were spilling from the gallery doorway and people were moving inside.

She took some photographs of the outside of the gallery with its festive decorations from across the road. Then she walked out from the pavement and over to the gallery entrance. She was strangely nervous. She didn't know anyone, but all she had to do was move around and talk to people and take photos. It wasn't difficult, but her chest was tight with anticipation. She made a deliberate effort to smile, took a breath and stepped inside.

Without people in it, the gallery must have been a wide, brightly lit space with a stripped-back oak floor and white walls hung with a great variety of paintings. As it was, there was hardly room to breathe for bodies and the scent of perfumes and pastries. A lot of people had clearly been invited for the evening's event; everyone was well-dressed, and an excited murmur hung over the crowd. There was a table at the far end with a selection of canapés and two waitresses pouring glasses of sparkling champagne.

Meg wasn't quite sure where to start. Her jersey dress that she thought so suitable seemed suddenly drab and not quite up to the occasion. Her bag was bulky with her work equipment, so unlike the tiny jewelled clutch bags the other women were carrying. Her confidence faltered, but she was here to work and that was what she would do. She decided to have a glass of champagne first to steady her nerves and allow her to walk around chatting to the guests and gauging their reaction to the artist's work. She hadn't even asked the community mag girl who the artist of the evening was. How silly of her. Never mind, she' soon get all the details. First of all, the champagne.

There was a bit of queue for the drinks. A tall man was standing in her way with his back to her, surrounded by a gaggle of friends talking to him. She had the fleeting impression that he wasn't happy with all the attention, when he turned around and the world stopped. It was Garth.

She stood frozen on her heels and stared into his dark blue eyes. She was reminded of the first time they'd met, because the vulnerability she'd seen in them was still there. He froze, too, and looked at her. They might have stayed like that for all eternity, except that an enthusiastic person behind her knocked her flying straight into Garth's arms.

His embrace was at once hard and strong and tender. Her nerve-endings were aflame, and did she imagine the brush of his lips on her brow as he steadied her? He put her there safely but didn't let his grip on her lessen. She felt the heat of the circle of his hand on her arm just above the elbow. Someone was speaking but she didn't hear what they said. She saw only him and her heart sang.

Then they were moving through the gallery, guests and faces turned to them in query, but Garth didn't answer them and Meg had no need to. She let him lead the way to a room off to the side. There was a moment to realise that all the art on the walls that evening was his. Why hadn't she seen that when she'd arrived? It all slotted into place in the blink of an eye. Garth was the special artist of the evening — the creative person she was to interview, and the walls were draped in his work, both light and dark, full of carefree beauty and darkly brooding landscapes. She held her breath and only let it out once the door was shut on the noisy chatter.

Neither spoke for a moment. Then they both moved at the same secor towards the other. There was no n for words as their bodies spoke inst

269

All the anguish and torment and doubt were extinguished by a searching kiss that heated them and healed them and lit a new fire within.

'I've missed you so much,' Meg whispered against his jaw, reaching up to stroke his skin in wonder.

'I've been a fool,' Garth groaned and pulled her against him feverishly for more kisses and caresses.

'No, I've been horribly full of foolish pride,' Meg said, wanting to take the blame, letting him stop her words with his mouth as it hardened and demanded of her what she wanted, *needed* to give to him.

'Meg, my darling Meg, can you forgive me for letting you go? For not trying harder to stop you leaving?'

'Only if you forgive me for not letting you share my feelings and worries about Phillip. I should've told you I'd seen him that day at the barbecue. I was wrong to keep it from you. What can o to put things right?'

et me love you. Come home with

me to Winter Farm and be my wife.' Garth stroked her hair and cupped her face to kiss her tenderly.

'You bought Primrose Cottage. I thought that meant you wanted me never to return,' Meg said, and her voice broke on a cry which was both happy and slightly sad.

'My darling, I bought it to keep it for you,' Garth laughed softly. 'I couldn't bear anyone else but you and Katie to live in it. I think I hoped if I kept it safely for you, then you'd eventually return to me.'

'Did you just propose to me?' Meg asked, catching up with his previous words. 'Because if you did, then the answer is yes, yes, yes. I'll marry you and we'll live happily ever after at Winter Farm.'

Garth gave a whoop and swept her off her feet and carried her around the small room while she pretended to kick and yell. The door opened and Gilda Mable walked in. Garth put Meg down and looked sheepish. Gilda smiled slowly.

'This is where you've got to. You

know, the guests are asking where you are. Hello, Meg. We haven't met, but I've heard you mentioned by Tabitha Shaw. Sorry, was I interrupting something?' Her eyes twinkled.

'We're leaving, Gilda. I don't care whether I sell any paintings or not. I want to take my fiancée and pick up my new daughter and get back to Devon tonight.'

Gilda put her palm up. 'Congratulations to both of you. But you made a promise to me, Garth. We're here now, aren't we? A compromise, then. Another hour and then you can leave. What do you say?'

'Plus I have an article to write,' Meg added. 'I'm meant to be interviewing you and photographing the paintings. I can't let my editor down.'

'Very well,' Garth said, taking the opportunity to kiss her again in spite of Gilda's raised brows. 'I'll give the interview and I'll talk to Gilda's guests, but there will be a special announcement this evening. The artist is getting married, and it's a celebration!'

# 16

'I want the fairy to sit at the top of the tree.'

Katie waved the doll in front of Ben's nose. It was a lovely confection of plastic, blonde hair, frothy white tulle, and silver wings with lots and lots of glitter. Katie had made the doll's costume at school and was very proud of it.

'Surely we should put the star on top. It's more traditional,' Ben teased her lazily, poking her middle with the large tinfoil-wrapped shape. It, too, had been made by Katie, and up until yesterday it had been her favourite for the top position on the Christmas tree.

Poppy gave a bark of agreement from her place lying in front of the fireplace. She was a fully grown dog now, and a working one at that. But she was also Ben's pet and followed him everywhere.

'We put the star on top of the tree last year, so why not give the fairy top billing this year?' Meg suggested, coming into the room with a tray of hot chocolate drinks.

'If this Christmas is as good as last year's, it's going to be fantastic,' Garth said, joining his wife on the sofa to watch the two put up the decorations.

Meg and Garth shared a conspiratorial smile. It was amazing to think a whole year had gone by since she'd literally bumped into Garth at the art gallery and accepted his proposal. She remembered how they'd hurried from the party as soon as Gilda would let them and gone back to her flat in Tottenham. It was too late to leave for Devon and they had tiptoed in and made up for all the lost weeks. The next day they had taken Katie and driven home to the farm.

Meg sold the flat to her neighbour's son, much to the old lady's delight. He and his girlfriend were able to look after her and she was never lost for companionship. In the end, Meg was glad to be rid of it. Too many memories, both good and bad. Primrose Cottage they had kept. She ran it as a holiday cottage and they already had a returning couple on their second short break there. Meg was sure it would become a firm favourite with many; it was such a dear little house. She didn't miss living there at all though. The many locks had been removed and replaced with one sturdy bolt, but she couldn't forget how uneasy she'd felt there when Phillip was haunting her. She reminded herself that he was an ocean away and nowadays she rarely thought about him.

'Are you going to visit your family over the holidays?' Garth asked Ben.

'Yeah, I said I'd pop in over for New Year. Brian's managed to get a new job, which is great, and Mum's a lot happier. You don't want me to move out, do you?' There was a hint of panic in the last question.

Meg touched his arm. 'Don't be daft.

You'll always have that bedroom here to come home to. Besides, what would Garth do without all the new information you bring back to the running of the farm?'

Ben was enrolled in college, studying business management and agriculture. In his holidays he lived at the farm and worked alongside Garth and Alex, putting his new knowledge into practice. The college wasn't far from his family, and while he was happy living in a student residence it meant he could visit on weekends to see his mum and step-dad and little sister.

A long, shrill cry rent the air.

'I'll get him,' Garth said. 'He doesn't nap for long, does he?'

'I'll help,' Katie shouted, throwing the fairy doll down and running after him. 'Tom loves me cuddling him when he wakes up.'

Garth waited for her and they both went up the stairs to fetch the baby. He lifted his son up from the Moses basket and cradled him. Katie crooned to her little brother. Garth smiled. His wish for a large family had come true. Ben was like a son to him and he hoped very much that he would want to help run the farm after college was finished. Garth intended to give him part ownership in due course. Katie was very much his daughter and she called him Dad very affectionately. Baby Tom was a delight even if he exhausted both his parents on a daily basis. Meg hinted she wanted more children too. There was no anxiety now for the future of Winter Farm. There were enough Winters to guarantee someone from the family would protect this land down the generations.

And most of all there was Meg. His beautiful wife was all he wanted and needed. She was the kindest person in the world and the love and passion he felt for her only increased every day of their married lives. On occasion, he noted a shadow in her expression and knew that she still wondered about Phillip and whether he might return. It was one tiny blight in their life together.

Downstairs there was a burst of laughter and the sound of children yelling. 'Jane's here!' Katie cried and ran ahead of him down the stairs to find her best friend.

'Oh let me hold this handsome chap.' Tabby reached for Tom and pecked a kiss at Garth's cheek. 'Thanks for inviting us all for Christmas dinner. I've brought extra food in case there isn't enough. Maurice, where's the hamper, darling? Have you left it in the car? Jacob, run out and get it and take Ellen with you. What do you mean, you can't find your coat? Never mind that now.'

Meg came out to greet her friend, and Garth and Maurice escaped into the garden on the pretence of putting the festive lights on the trees. In the kitchen not a single surface was bare of food and plates, and the enormous turkey was already roasting and filling the room with nostalgic smells. The hamper arrived, swung between the children, and Meg helped Tabby to unload it. Tom sat in his baby bouncer and watched with solemn, round eyes.

'How's your book going?' Tabby asked, unwrapping the glazed ham and setting it on a plate. 'You must be nearly finished it by now.'

'Not really,' Meg said ruefully. 'Why I ever thought writing a novel would be easier than commissioned articles, I don't know. It's nearly there but I can't quite finish it. There are loose ends that I can't seem to quite tie up.'

'Loose ends? I've no idea what you're talking about, but I'm sure you'll get it finished because you are very talented, my girl. Oh, look at this Devonshire honey. Not really seasonal, but delicious all the same. Now, shall I get the kids to set the table?'

Meg nodded and let Tabby direct the operations. She couldn't explain it anyway. Her book was coming along nicely, but the love story wouldn't conclude properly. She put it to the back of her mind. It was Christmas Day, after all, and there was so much chaos in the house that she was needed on all fronts to keep the day going smoothly.

She hardly heard the bell when it rang. Then Jane and Katie were tugging at her apron and telling her there was a lady who wanted to speak to her. Meg frowned. Who could be at the door on Christmas Day? She sent the kids off with packets of chocolate buttons to share with the others and went to find out.

Leila Graham smiled. She was impeccably turned out in a cream cashmere coat and matching hat and leather gloves and boots. Her hair was neatly twisted into long curls that must have taken a good hairdresser hours to fix into place. She looked tanned and relaxed and exotically out of place on Meg's front doorstep.

'Come in, please,' Meg said and beckoned her inside out of the cold day. She led Leila into the front room, away from the swell of sound in the living room.

'I'm sorry, Meg; you have guests for Christmas and I'm intruding.' Meg had forgotten how wonderfully smooth Leila's voice was.

'Not at all. I'm surprised to see you again, but it's lovely all the same. Can I offer you a drink? Or would you like to join us all in the other room?'

A look of almost horror passed across Leila's face at that suggestion. No, she assured Meg, she wouldn't stay long, and this room was perfect for what she had to tell her. Intrigued, Meg sank down into the nearest armchair and Leila did the same, her long elegant legs slanted to one side as she perched on the chair next to Meg's.

'I'd forgotten it was Christmas. You will find that hard to believe, but I've been out in the Bahamas in the glorious sunshine for so long and I've been commuting to the States back and forth a lot recently.' Leila smiled at Meg. 'You're wondering why I've come to tell you that.'

'To be honest, yes,' Meg replied.

'I'm back in England to visit my father. But I made a little detour to see you. The reason I'm here is because of Phillip.'

Meg's breath caught in her chest. He still cast a shadow on her life. But Leila was shaking her head gently. 'You have no reason to be worried about Phillip. That's partly what I came to say. You won't believe this, Meg, but Phillip and I are together again.'

There was a glow to Leila that Meg noticed now. The tension around her mouth that Meg had seen on her last visit was gone. She looked younger and even more stunning than before.

'You went back to him?' Meg didn't want to sound rude with astonishment but it was hard to hide it.

Leila laughed. 'You're amazed. Well, so am I in a way. Phillip's changed. I don't think you would recognise him now. He is self-aware and contrite and a much-improved husband. The little gifts and the charm are there once more, but it's better — more . . . *real* than before. If that makes sense?'

'Are you sure?'

'Yes, I'm positive. He came to visit me in the Bahamas and met a therapist. This wonderful woman healed him. When he visited me a second time I fell in love with him all over again. Yes, he still likes to be the boss, but now he can take no for an answer. He knows I need my personal space. It's hard for him, but we're working on these issues together. And I know my marriage will be stronger for it.'

At Leila's words and conviction, it was as if a shadow lifted from Meg. The flicker in the corner of her vision that hovered over her vanished. Phillip had his happy-ever-after too. She could move on without him in her thoughts.

'He asked me to speak to you,' Leila went on. 'He is still over in America and he knew you wouldn't be happy to see him. But he wants to get his lawyer in touch with yours.'

'Why?' Meg asked.

Beyond the room, there was a shriek of laughter and the wail of a party hooter.

'He wishes to make Katie his heir. There will be no more children for us. Phillip doesn't want to be a father to his daughter in the traditional sense, but he wants to contribute to her welfare. So, she will inherit all his wealth one day.'

Meg began to speak but Leila shook her head. 'Please, Meg, allow him this one request. He knows he cannot make up to you for all his terrible behaviour. He knows, too, that he would make an awful day-to-day father to Katie. But this is his way of saying he cares for her. Please?'

'Okay. If that's what he wants, then yes. When Katie reaches eighteen she may have her own views on it, but until then, yes let his lawyer speak to mine.' Meg wasn't sure what she felt about all this, but it was time to forgive and forget and to move on. Garth had managed to make his peace with Anna's memory. Couldn't Meg be generous, too, and allow Phillip his remorse and gesture? Yes, she could. Meg was strong now. She grew in strength every day in her love for Garth and her family.

'I must go up to London now. My father will be waiting for me,' Leila said, rising gracefully.

'How will you celebrate today?' Meg asked.

'Dinner at the Ritz and a supper dance at my friend's house.'

Meg could quite imagine what Leila's friend's house would look like. A massive mansion, no doubt. But she didn't envy her dinner at one of the most expensive hotels in London or her celebrity lifestyle one little bit. She let Leila out and waved goodbye until her car had gone. Then she went to join the mayhem in the living room. There was a game of charades underway and Katie was dishing out paper party hats. Tom was sitting on Maurice's knee, wearing a green and gold hat and looking surprised. Poppy was jumping up like a naughty puppy at Ellen, who had a plate of Christmas cookies, and Jacob and William were taking advantage of her distraction to steal the cookies from the other side. Ben was standing on a stool trying to staple the fairy doll to the top of the tree under Tabby's shouted instructions.

'Who was at the door?' Garth asked, coming over to her and putting his arm around her.

She felt sheltered there. 'It was Leila,' she said. 'I'll tell you all about it when the noise dies down.'

'That'll be a while then,' Garth replied with a grin. 'You look . . . better somehow.'

'I feel better,' Meg agreed. 'It was something that Leila said.'

'Mummy, the turkey needs you.' Katie's muffled shout came from the kitchen along with the distinctive smell of burning bird.

With a shriek, Meg and Tabby both ran to the oven. Maurice grimaced at Garth and Garth decided it was the moment to open the box of emergency mince pies. The children and dog agreed. Luckily the turkey was all right, and after basting, it was announced by

Meg that Christmas dinner would soon be served. There was a scattering of the families to wash hands and get ready.

Garth and Meg were left alone for a few peaceful moments. Meg snapped her fingers in revelation. That was it. She knew now how to tie up the loose end in her love story. She gave Garth a long, heartfelt kiss. Tomorrow she'd finish her book and type in the title: *To Love Again*.

## THE END

We do hope that you have enjoyed reading this large print book.

Did you know that all of our titles are available for purchase?

We publish a wide range of high quality large print books including:
**Romances, Mysteries, Classics**
**General Fiction**
**Non Fiction and Westerns**

Special interest titles available in large print are:
**The Little Oxford Dictionary**
**Music Book, Song Book**
**Hymn Book, Service Book**

Also available from us courtesy of Oxford University Press:
**Young Readers' Dictionary**
**(large print edition)**
**Young Readers' Thesaurus**
**(large print edition)**

For further information or a free brochure, please contact us at:
**Ulverscroft Large Print Books Ltd.,**
**The Green, Bradgate Road, Anstey,**
**Leicester, LE7 7FU, England.**
**Tel:** (00 44) **0116 236 4325**
**Fax:** (00 44) **0116 234 0205**

# GIRL WITH A GOLD WING

## Jill Barry

It's the 1960s, and Cora Murray dreams of taking to the skies — so when her father shows her a recruitment advertisement for air hostesses, she jumps at the chance to apply. Passing the interview with flying colours, she throws herself into her training, where she is quite literally swept off her feet by First Officer Ross Anderson. But whilst Ross is charming and flirtatious, he's also engaged — and Cora's former boyfriend Dave is intent on regaining her affections . . .

# THE SURGEON'S MISTAKE

## Chrissie Loveday

Matti Harper has been in love with Ian Faulkner since their school days. He is now an eminent cardiac surgeon, she his theatre nurse. Ian has finally fallen in love — the trouble is, it's with Matti's flatmate Lori! But whilst a heartbroken Matti prepares to be their bridesmaid, Lori is being suspiciously flirtatious with another man. How can Matti tell Ian without appearing to be jealous? Best man Sam Grayling tries to help, but only succeeds in sending things from bad to worse . . .